Mike:

I hope "journey" you are about to begin with "Krizmerian Logic".

I thought you would find of interest the sales process set forth in the book as well as appreciate the connection between leadership and salesmanship.

I wish you great success in your career. I know you will have a bright future in Nashville.

Best Regards,

ENJOY!!

Shelly

Krizmerian Logic

SHELDON L. KRIZELMAN

Copyright © 2002 by Sheldon L. Krizelman. All rights reserved. No part of this book may be reproduced or transmitted in any form or by any means without the express written permission of the author.

TABLE OF CONTENTS

I.	ACKNOWLEDGMENTS	7
II.	PREFACE/PROLOGUE/INTRODUCTION	9
III.	SALESMANSHIP AS LEADERSHIP	11
IV.	SALESMANSHIP AND LEADERSHIP	14
V.	SALES PHILOSOPHY AND PROCESS	43
VI.	ACCEPTANCE SPEECH FOR PHILIP KOTLER AWARD FOR EXCELLENCE IN HEALTHCARE MARKETING	46
VII.	PERSONAL VIEWS OF LEADERSHIP	54
VIII.	THE "STORIES" SEEING THE DRAMA THAT OTHER PEOPLE MISS ...AND SELLING HOT HOPE	59
IX.	ABOUT THE AUTHOR	131

I. ACKNOWLEDGMENTS

There are so many people to thank because over many years my family, friends and professional colleagues encouraged me to put down in writing my sales philosophy/process and the numerous "stories" associated with the multitude of marketing projects and related activities.

First, I must thank my loving wife, Patricia Kraft Krizelman, who continually encouraged me to follow through and put these thoughts in writing. Also, she tirelessly performed the invaluable work of editing the text of the manuscript. Noted author educator and national leadership "guru," Terry Deal, Ph.D., not only gave me the encouragement to write the book but also the helpful advice on how to get the writing done.

I want to thank my terrific daughters – Lora Sue Krizelman and Kimberly Ann Krizelman, who always seemed to understand why I was traveling on business while they were growing up and, more recently, for their strong encouragement to complete this book. I also want to thank them for their review of the manuscript as well as for Kim's creative design of the cover of the book and Lora's contribution to the text of the cover. Also, a special thank you to my wonderful brother, Al Krizelman, who is a man of unparalleled wisdom.

Obviously, I must thank my business partners, Robert D. Huseby and Thomas Singleton, who not only provided the business environment to make our companies successful, but were "participants" in the numerous "stories" set forth herein. Also, I want to thank John Siedlecki, Executive Vice President of Marketing for Quorum Health Resources, who always encouraged me to write this book and has a brilliant marketing mind that so understands what this book is all about. Additional appreciation goes to James Stokes, former president of Quorum Health Resources, who always respected the marketing process. A thank you must be extended to Gayle Mitchell who was my administrative assistant for nearly 20 years and helped maintain the integrity of the multiple phases of the sales process.

I would like to single out Joel C. Gordon who has not only been a wonderful friend but a great role model and mentor. Additionally, I would like to single out Ken Melkus, a great friend and a trusted advisor.

Sincere appreciation must be extended to both Dan Baker, Ph.D., Director of Family Business at Canyon Ranch in Tucson, Arizona, as well as Dan Parker, a partner in the executive search firm of Baker-Parker in Atlanta. Both men encouraged me to write this book and they remain my close friends.

I also want to thank the numerous healthcare marketing and operations professionals I had the privilege of working with over the past 30 years. I learned so much from all those colleagues who are too numerous to mention by name.

I must thank Candace Holloran who typed this manuscript and always maintained her patience and professionalism and her constant high standards of quality.

Most of all, I want to thank all the wonderful clients who I learned so much from and who made everything possible!!

II. PREFACE/PROLOGUE/INTRODUCTION

Over many years my family, friends and professional colleagues have encouraged me to write a book which details my sales philosophy and process and also sets forth the numerous "stories" associated with all of these transactions over the past 30 years.

I decided to write this book because I believe my sales philosophy and process could be useful to others. Also, I see the direct important relationship between salesmanship and leadership and have decided to share my thoughts on this subject so others can apply these principles in all aspects of their life.

Additionally, I truly believe I see the drama that other people miss. Also, I believe in the concept of selling hot hope. Accordingly, I have set forth 49 "stories" which illustrate that point. As I review these stories, it would appear that some have a significant marketing/sales principle behind them and the balance are more "pop culture" in that they are reflective of a traveling executive going from one community to another to "do deals." The 49 stories are merely some examples of the hundreds of stories that could have been set forth in this book. They are not organized in any chronological order but rather are placed in a very random manner without reference to either time or subject. As you read the stories, on numerous occasions, I make reference to Robert D. Huseby who was my long time business partner and a principal and founder of our three companies. Additionally, I make reference to Tom Singleton who was our chief financial officer of all three companies and member of the board of all three companies. Also, Tom Beavor is mentioned often in his role as senior vice president of marketing of Hospital Management Professionals (HMP). I believe this book is both a business book with important sales/marketing principles and a collection of "pop culture" stories.

In summary, the book includes my sales philosophy and process which is the cornerstone of why I wrote this book. It also contains the detailed connection I see between salesmanship *and* leadership as well as a description of salesmanship *as* leadership. It also includes my personal view of leadership as set forth in a talk I gave in May of 1994 to the leadership class at the Executive MBA Program of the Owen Graduate School of Management of Vanderbilt University.

I've also enclosed a copy of the outline of my acceptance speech for the Philip Kotler Award for Excellence in Healthcare Marketing which I delivered in June of 1996 at a symposium of the Healthcare Marketing Division of the American Marketing Association in Boston. As you may know, Philip Kotler, Ph.D., is a nationally renown marketing professor on the faculty of the Kellogg School at Northwestern University.

Enjoy!! I hope you find your journey rewarding.

III. SALESMANSHIP AS LEADERSHIP

Few businesses today are the small "mom and pop" enterprises of the past. Rather, they are large, complex organizations with operations scattered across geographic and national boundaries. The need for consistency, standardization, and control in such intricate, often tangled, enterprises breeds an impersonal process called management. Managers are rightfully obsessed with efficiency, accountability, supervision and results. They hold things together through rules, regulations, commands and data. Managers focus on telling people what to do and watching to make sure that it's done.

While all this is important, it leaves out a critical variable – people. Even as organizations grow in size, complexity and sophistication, business transactions are inevitably carried out by human beings. People are only partially governed by rational logic; they are more strongly motivated by needs, moods and intrinsic desires. They crave relationships and want work to have some meaning, purpose and sizzle. This is where leadership fills a void that management can rarely touch. Leaders give equal weight to the task and to people. They pursue profits through people, by engaging in the process of selling. They sell visions, ideas, stories and other intangibles. As one chief executive observed: "My job? I sell hot hope."

Leadership is inherently a process of salesmanship. Not salesmanship in the stereotypical sense of the hawker of used cars who judges, exhorts, lies and manipulates to do a deal. That image distorts and demeans what selling is all about. Fusing the two ideas of Salesmanship and Leadership offers a novel view based on the following precepts:

> 1. *Leaders pursue value.* The first obligation is to ensure that products or services offer something desirable to someone.

> 2. *Within the company, operations and sales cannot be partitioned.* People in production and those who represent the product or service directly are part of a seamless process. Selling internally and selling externally are complimentary functions.

3. *Nothing gets sold outside the "moment of truth"* where a company representative actually touches a customer or client intellectually, emotionally, or physically – a handshake consummates a deal.

4. *All business transactions are human transactions.* People do business with other people. As a result, building and maintaining relationships carries a very high premium.

5. *Economies of scale potentially have mutual benefit.* Both employees and clients can benefit as the company grows.

6. *All business transactions are emotional.* They require people on both sides who are in touch with their emotions and are willing to imbue the deal with a personal touch.

7. *Networks, not statistics, are vital to seeing where the most promising leads exist and getting things done.*

8. *Internal cohesiveness across various functions insures the delivery of a top quality product or service.* Without spiritual glue the enterprise falls apart.

9. *Frequency of closure* rather than panic selling due to fear should dominate the process.

10. *Listening to find out what people need as opposed to what they might want is a crucial leadership skill.* Action without discovery – a solid understanding of what's really going on is usually counterproductive.

11. *Selling is selling*, a value that must permeate the culture applying to all transactions.

12. *Walking away from a deal you can't handle is as important as consummating a deal you know something about.* Knowing when to hold and when to fold is a prime requisite in leadership judgment.

13. *Without closure and commitment, nothing ever happens.* Closing a deal is the test of a good salesperson. Securing shared commitment to a course of action is the stuff of effective leadership.

The ability to sell is the world's most beneficial skill – *no exceptions*. If you compare two leaders with equal talents and one is demonstrably more successful than the other, you will inevitably find that the differentiating factor is salesmanship – *no exceptions*.

IV. SALESMANSHIP AND LEADERSHIP

When I think about salesmanship and leadership, the first thing I see is a real parallel. What does a leader do? A leader sets the vision, a leader communicates the vision, a leader charts the course, and a leader makes sure there are specific steps to get from the starting point to the completion of the vision. One of the things that jumps out at me is what leaders do - the hard stuff. Leaders understand in their soul that whatever they are going to do, if it's worthwhile, is going to be hard. If it's not hard, you're doing something wrong. You're not even in the game if it's not hard. Above all, leaders communicate an expectation that hard is good and that pushing through those resistances or barriers is what it's all about. In the sales process, all these steps are in place, from the vision, the course, the steps, to the consummation of transaction - all these things – as well as the understanding above all that it is going to be difficult. When it gets the most difficult, you probably are right at the critical point of success or failure and that's when you have to get real, real focused. This is a parallel I see between salesmanship and leadership: the leader who understands that hard is good is a great salesman. In fact, I always say, "If it ain't hard, there isn't any money in it, and this is getting pretty hard, so we must be getting close to the money."

I'm going to talk now for a minute about the things that make a salesperson successful. The first thing, ironically, that makes him successful is the understanding that when he is sitting down in front of a client, and the client is taking the time to talk to him and knows why he's there, the client has already admitted to him that there's a problem and that they can't figure out the answer to it by themselves. Once they "admit" they have a problem that they can't solve by themselves, they're already in a position of vulnerability. Sales is about emotion, people buying from people and closing. One of the biggest problems is that the client's emotion can enter the sales process as the enemy, because he is fundamentally saying, "I can't fix my problem by myself, and I've admitted that to you because here you are. But don't get carried away, because I am the man, and I have a big ego. So we're going to do this dance now, and this courtship is a way that you pay homage to me. Yes, I have admitted to you I have a problem and I don't know how to solve it, but if I don't like your solutions or I'm not comfortable with them, I'm going to buck you all the way." Even though this response is probably because you're the expert in selling (your product or service) and know what they need, they are reluctant to accept that. What makes the sales process a challenge is getting the client to accept the right solution when they don't want to. In other words, getting people to want to do what you want them to do. That is really why a salesperson must develop strong leadership skills and become a leader, because, effectively, for a moment in time, I believe that when he comes to a potential client, he is really becoming a de facto leader of that client's company. He's working with someone at a high level. If he is working with a board or if he is working with the CEO, then he actually is the interim de facto CEO, leading them through tough decision making to a solution for that moment in time, and then he leaves.

That's in the business-to-business arena. In the consumer arena, any company that sells hard products, that sells goods, must understand that the following model doesn't work: we sell goods (by internet, direct mail advertising, or in a showroom), people buy the goods, that's the deal. The customer buys the goods, he gets them and leaves. You're not looking at a successful company. Everyone today understands that it's all about value-add, it's all about the whole buying experience of the consumer. It isn't just the product that's being purchased, it's everything that surrounds the product. Dell Computers is a great example. It sells, supports, services, anticipates, etc. What Dell has become very, very good at is implementing this sales concept - the "Krizmerian" sales process – not simply running a promotion, answering a client's call and taking orders.

I recently bought a Dell computer. When I called the Dell salesperson, their process was very clear to me. He asked, "What is your goal eventually? Is this a family computer? Or is this for an individual?" We talked about what I needed. Then he basically outlined Dell's process, i.e., you will need to get these certain components and we'll talk about the components and everything. What he was doing was outlining the process to me through to closure. When he had established what the goal was going to be, he then established the course to the goal. He knew he had to meet my needs in terms of particular hardware and service, as well as all the accompanying details. He simply led me through the "Krizmerian" sales process. I think this is very different from how companies behaved years ago when they really were order takers. The Dell salesperson was an intelligent person who had a very thorough knowledge of the product and was very good at selling, i.e., walking me from start to finish. I think that is a major change in the last ten or so years. Companies have clearly realized that you must have a sales process, even in high volume consumer products. The closer you get to a true sales process to bring closure to the purchase, the more successful you'll be.

In service businesses, such as the great examples of Southwest Airlines and Starbucks Coffee, the sale, the actual exchange of money between the seller and the consumer, is a different kind of transaction than that of selling a hard asset. There is an element in their sales process similar to selling a hard asset, but not really. When someone is coming in a store to buy a cup of coffee, there really is no negotiation; you really are taking an order. So where does the selling enter in? Is this just promotion? I don't think so. I think it's really the classic example of leadership as salesmanship. What makes Starbucks different? Is it really just about the promotion? Is it just the brand? Is it the fact that the product tastes a little better? I think it's really a whole aura, a whole sensation and phenomenon that's created in the mind of the consumer and, yeah, it's the product, no question about it. But as good a product as Starbucks coffee is (and it's my personal favorite, and it IS better), what leads me to a Starbucks is that a leader/salesman has created a culture. The selling process that occurs in this kind of organization really takes place before the money changes hands by means of the creation of a culture. Basically, the employees have bought into the culture of the business model of the company which is not only to sell coffee, but to treat their consumers in a certain way when they come in the door and to do that consistently with every consumer in every location. No matter which Starbucks the customer goes to, he's going to have not just a cup of coffee, but an experience. The leadership and salesmanship is exemplified from the CEO down the chain of command to the people at the coffee counter where the selling takes place. A leader must imbue that understanding into the culture of the company, and that takes selling. Without a strong leader you'll just end up with employees who say, "I just want to sell coffee here at Starbucks."

There are really two dimensions of sales. In the B-to-B world, sales is really the quintessential and definable step by step sales process that brings closure to multi-million or billion dollar transactions. The sales process is less visible in the internal process of sales, which actually may be the more difficult. It may be a greater leadership challenge in some ways, because if you think about it, the CEO of a company's business model is more dependent on his sales ability than in any other business. Effectively, what he must do is sell his entire employee base (which may be 100,000 if you are an airline) at one time on the business model. He must take all the members of the company family through a process and set up the goal, whether it's a flight attendant or an equity holder in the company. This is what he has to do to make transactions happen every day. In essence, what the leader of an organization knows is that, in terms of the sales process, "qualifying the lead" really means qualifying the employee. The company's goal is to get the employees to buy into their business model and to lead them to the goal which, in essence, is the company's objective: putting the employees into the mindset to satisfy their client base. It's really about qualifying the right talent for the organization.

The next piece is the conceptual presentation of the business model to the employees and in turn getting buy-in from this massive base of people. Closure comes when the employee accepts a position and an offer and agrees to conduct business to satisfy the consumer in a certain way. Then the closure is ultimately the payoff, i.e., watching the equity in the company increase. That's the internal sale.

Then there's the external promotion. In the continuum of companies there are those that sell coffee as simply a transaction. There's really not necessarily a sale to be made just because somebody comes into the door. That's one end of the continuum. The higher end of the continuum is a company, like a resort or an on-line computer seller in which, unlike the thinking of a company that says, "We've done our promotion and we're ready to take your order," the sales process begins when a salesperson says, "We have you on the phone; now we have that sales process outlined." It's very careful, and the steps are very methodical. They're all designed to lead the prospect to closure on the product and increase of closure leads to equity.

Regardless of the kind of organization, in many companies today the following is one of the most important themes in leadership and salesmanship. Everyone would like to think - no matter what their company, or their enterprise, or their product, or their social mission - we all like to think in our heart of hearts - that what we can do will be so clever and will make our product so special and so out in front and so much different that for a moment in time we effectively create a monopoly, until someone catches up. In the old days, one drug, penicillin, got a patent on it and it was a breakthrough, and for ten years you have a heyday, you own it. If you have the first computer chip, that's a breakthrough computer chip. Well, that's great, but let's look at how it exists. Everyone knows that business cycles, product cycles, life cycles have shortened dramatically, so if you believe you're going to capture a monopoly because of the specialization of your product and your technical advantage, you're pretty much in dreamland. AMD introduced the first "gigahertz" chip and within probably a month or two I'm sure Intel had a "gigahertz" plus point one.

More often than not, what you're selling, whether it's Purdue chicken or something else, is almost always a commodity. If it's not a commodity, it's only going to have a special advantage for a short period of time. That's the boat we're all in. Unless you're NASA and you're selling space shuttle flights, there's always competition. That's why a leader, a salesperson, is going to set the tone. I think Purdue chicken is a classic example because really what the consumer buys is not the chicken -

what they buy is the leader. The chicken is good, Starbucks coffee is good, and I can tell you that Purdue chicken sometimes tastes a little better to me than all the other chickens that are out there. Other times I'll say to my wife, this chicken is pretty good tonight but why didn't you get Purdue, and she'll say it is Purdue. So much of the taste is in my mindset that when I see that I'm eating Purdue chicken, I'm thinking about how much I like Frank Purdue and that chicken tastes better. If I don't know it and don't see the label, I can't tell that I'm eating Purdue chicken. No offense to Starbucks coffee, but the same might be true. What I'm buying is Frank Purdue, is the Starbucks hipness, the cool feeling, that I'm in there - not just for a cup of coffee, I'm in there for an experience. I'd be interested to see the results if you asked 1,000 people who enjoyed Starbucks coffee inside of Starbucks - sitting down with a friend, with the sunlight coming through the glass, in a good location in Manhattan: "How do you like Starbucks as compared to . . .?" I'd be willing to bet the approval or satisfaction rating from that 1,000 people, who actually sat and chatted and drank, is going to be very high as compared to a 1,000 people who went in and got a cup in styrofoam to go. I bet that if nine out of ten in the first group would say it's the best, that only five out of ten, at most, in the second group would say it's the best, because the second group is just buying a cup of coffee - they haven't really been sold. The people who have been sold sit down and make it an experience several days a week.

    Dell makes a fabulous computer, but so do nine other companies. They all have the same components made by the same manufacturers. These companies don't manufacture any of the components, not really. There may be a few things they manufacture, but they buy most from Intel, they buy them from Motorola, they buy them from hard drive manufacturers, and then they assemble them, and they are all marketing organizations. The only thing that makes Dell computer neater than Compaq or neater than Hewlett Packard is that Michael Dell is the only person, except for Steve Jobs at Apple, who, if you asked ten people who the CEO of Dell computer is, they would know it is this handsome young guy named Michael Dell. You just get a feeling when you see him that says, "I like him, I want to line up behind that guy." Because he is a leader. The same thing with Jobs. What you're buying is the leader. If you lift the tin cup and look underneath, what you're looking at is a commodity in all these situations.

In leadership and salesmanship what comes to my mind, based on my experience, is the fact that the most important dimension in selling which relates to the leadership of an organization, is one thing and one thing first and foremost - the empowerment of dare. On the subject of the empowerment of dare, I think what that is simply saying - which is very powerful – is that as a leader you have to transfer courage and absolute confidence to your sales people. Of course, that ultimately permeates through the entire organization. If anyone is going to be successful, very simply, they have to absolutely have no fear. Fear cannot be part of their decision making process. It can't be part of their tactical process. And actually they have to feel good. They have to like the feeling of getting a "no" because they were too bold. It's very simple. It's only an occasional adjustment if a salesperson says, "I was too bold two out of ten times and well, maybe that was one too many." He needs to be bold all the time. The fact is, if you take any organization doing significant transactions as deals, and if you look at their loss column, and you ask how many times did they lose because the client said they were just a little too bold or a little too rash, it's probably happened in one out of ten losses at most, and the other nine losses are because we didn't push the envelope.

Another important factor is leadership. Empowerment of dare is created when a culture says that losses through boldness are absolutely acceptable and, in fact, they are red badges of courage. Losses due to lack of dare and boldness are not acceptable. You are empowered to lose because of boldness - you don't have to check with anybody - be bold. There's basically two elements to bold behavior. One is simply being tenacious and persistent and moving to closure. The other element of boldness is belief in your product or service. This is where the synergy between operations and marketing comes into play. If we're going to be bold on the sales side and we're going to believe in our product, then we have to see the same boldness, like looking in the mirror, when we look at the operations job. No matter how tough the job, how tough the computer conversion or whatever it is the sales team is going to deliver for your client, if you believe that your client really has a tough problem and that there are few companies that could solve it, and we know the chance of their success is greatest with us, then we have an obligation to our client to sell to them or we are letting our client down as well.

The next subject is why do people buy things? This is so important because whatever the product is, it's pretty much a commodity. There's always at least two or three other flavors. And so ultimately somebody's buying something because of an emotional reason, and I don't care if its microchips or screws, there's an emotional reason. And that gets into the concept of hot hope. It's interesting in today's culture, in the year 2002, to look at how the world is transformed. For people who are fortunate to get a good education, to work hard and have a good career, the sky is the limit. Look at all of the devices that make our life better and more convenient, that free up our time, and we all have such an expectation for a better life. We all have an extremely high internal level of hope at this point. What we really want from anybody that sells us anything is that hot hope concept, because we really have expectations (a lot of it driven by information technology) that life gets better in quantum leaps. Not just a little bit better, but rapid, radical change monthly. On the news and in the paper you see 4,000 ways you can make your professional life better, through another service, an Internet-based service or any kind of service, then you see the same thing on the consumer side. That hope is critical and there's a huge dimension, a huge power behind that.

I'm going to go back to dare for one second. The hardest thing about dare is the sustaining of dare - how to maintain that culture of dare. If a company falls behind in its budget and says a particular account is one it really needs, maybe the company will bend just a little bit, and if it does it really selectively, maybe once or twice in a year, that might be okay, maybe. But it is such an insidious event, it's like a disease. You do it once and it's too easy to continue in that pattern. To be very conscious to never break the thrust of dare, to never break that tradition, is critical because the minute you compromise it you're in a vicious cycle downward and you no longer push the envelope. Frankly, there's a real irony to this. The person who dares the most, probably in most cases, appears to be the best choice to the client because when they ask, "How can you be so bold to want this deal structured a certain way?" The answer is, "Because it's the right way for you, client, or you will fail." How can they be so bold to want a 50% premium over their competition and, gosh, maybe it's because they're that much better, and you walk away with it. In the biotech world, Tissue Plasminogen Activator (TPA) was sold against Streptokinase, and after many studies and many years, it was finally shown that, despite their claims, they both were effective, yet the price for TPA was $2,000 versus $50 a dose for Streptokinase. When that product was launched and the follow-up research hadn't been done yet to support major mortality benefit claims, an awful lot of the reason the drug TPA was sold successfully is because it was priced 20 times above the competition and the world believed it must be good. And that's dare.

On the competition, everyone knows that . . . and this kind of segues from dare . . . the number one competitor to everyone selling anything is, of course, "no decision." That's why boldness and dare are so important as well. In a sales culture where leadership as salesmanship exists, what you do, if you do it right, is you breed warriors. There's a quote from Don Juan de Marco that is my personal favorite quote, which says "the difference between an ordinary man and a warrior is that an ordinary man sees everything as either a blessing or a curse, whereas a warrior sees everything as a challenge." It's a compliment when I tell someone they're a warrior. I pay that compliment to a human being maybe once in three years. I don't give that one out idly. I might say you're a superstar, you're a lot of things, that's just banter. What that quote says to me is, you are absolutely in control of your own destiny, your own fate. The minute we're saying the client is indecisive, or the competition is tough, or a product or service needs to be updated, you are in an ordinary man mode. A warrior just doesn't go there. A warrior just finds the path to success and frankly enjoys the problems, the bumps in the road, because without them, the warrior would be bored; it wouldn't be any fun.

No decision is the number one competitor. No decision is not in any way a failure on the client's part to be decisive, it's not a failure on the client's part because they wasted your time. The fact that they asked you in the first place means they had an intent, and no decision means that you just failed to implement the process. That's every B-to-B sales organization's number one competitor, number one challenge. And it's great news if you really think about it. That it's just you and the process, that's all there is. So it's like having an exclusive on the deal if you implement the process correctly.

If no decision really is the number one competitor, and no decision is a function of poor sales process, then that means that as good as we all believe we are in selling, and as good as we train our people, when there's a breakdown and it results in a no decision, there are a lot of steps that were missed even by the best professionals. Going back to basics, probably one of the reasons no decision happens is, a good salesperson knows their steps, he's going to qualify, he's going to make an initial visit with the decision maker, he's going to find out who the decision maker or makers are. But ultimately there's one guy pulling the trigger. A lot of people still miss that step. It's really easy to say, the number two guy is really the decision maker because he liked me, he talked to me, he told me that, but you know that, ultimately, he is not making the decision. We all get sucked into that over and over again. And it's a tough situation because that's where dare comes in. That's the first tough realization that I'm not at the decision maker. I haven't been granted access. Now am I just going to cease and desist or am I going to roll the dice and stick with the number two guy? If you roll the dice, you're going to lose or be in the no decision situation.

The next step, of course, especially in such large transactions where we're almost always involved in a group sales process, and we have a large group of stakeholders to sell, is to sell the concept first. We know ultimately that we're going to ask somebody for a check for a couple of million dollars and that they are going to focus on the services or the product and the cost. We all like to think that everyone thinks about return on investment. We do when we're selling things, but when we're buying things, we don't. We just see the cost. I think it is very interesting to look at a comparison of purchasing decisions in the business world of an individual, e.g., Mark Smith. How does Mark Smith's personal buying power impact how he buys as an executive for an oil company? Because we probably make a lot more purchasing decisions in our consumer life, we really focus on the cost. Other people focus on value and so when they pay, they understand the return is in the value. You really have to quickly sort out where your client is, and a lot of times they are on the cost side. If we don't do some sort of validation - a survey, an assessment or something - to show the return on investment, then what we're selling is, "here's this stuff and here's the enormous fee." We never get them to see the return which is why they are making the decision in the first place. That's where dare comes in again, because at least half of your clients are going to say yours is an evasive process and they would rather you give them some basic information and tell them where they should go. Whereas if you can create a process where you effectively become partners with your client for a short period of time, you become part of the fiber of their organization; you start to work together. That creates the right emotional setting to move forward and the opportunity to truly validate the ROI or invalidate the ROI. In this case the courageous salesperson says, I am cutting my losses and I'm leaving now because all I'm going to do is spend three more weeks of time and money and not sell this product. Therefore, I'll go to my next candidate who is ready and where I can show value. Because if I can't show value, I don't really have any business going after the potential new client. All that will do is damage my reputation and result in an unsatisfied client.

After the ROI, finally we come to the proposal presentation, which takes place in most companies today. So often, especially in a cooperative culture of marketing and operations, there can be some poisoning of the marketing discipline between these two functions. The marketing professional knows deals are not done by exchange of paper, deals are done through implementation of effective selling strategies and tactics and that's face to face. Worse case, it's on the telephone, but if we're reduced to exchanging documents and think we're selling, then we have missed the point. That's tough, too, because so many clients today are under so much time pressure they say just send me some documents and I'll give you a reaction, and that's death. So, moving from the survey to closure means another presentation, not an exchange of documents, but a face-to-face presentation. And then, most importantly, we've blown everything we've just covered if in step one we haven't outlined a decision making timetable and informed the client of our process, i.e., to figure out whether or not we can add value for their benefit and then establish a timetable that meets their needs and that they can agree to before they render their decision. It's difficult for some salespeople to tell a client in advance that they have an expectation of him, vis-à-vis his decision making timetable. They think that one-dimensional leadership is the sales force itself. They have to have a very strong leader who convinces them that the only unforgivable sin is lack of dare. It requires boldness and dare on the part of the sales executive to require a decision by the client within a certain timeframe.

There are two more major elements of leadership in the sales process, at least two. One element is leading the sales team. There has to be, as on every team, only one quarterback on the field at any one time, and everybody has to know clearly who the quarterback is that's calling the plays. So much selling today is done in team fashion because of the technical requirements of products and the realization that the person who knows how the computer box works is not necessarily the best salesperson. But the whole process can get really muddled if it isn't clear who is in charge of setting the sales tactics and strategies for making the tough calls.

The other element of leadership in the sales process is actually more fascinating. It is the fact that when you are dealing with large organizations and they have significant problems, you might be looking at an organization who may be searching for leadership. They may have a great affinity for your company if they see leadership qualities in their salesperson. In their mind they can adopt him as the leader in the moment. In organizations that are indecisive about major issues, a good sales team can create leadership.

In the hospital management business, I always knew when I did the best work that I'm capable of doing. One example was the best hospital that I ever worked with, in the best financial shape - which was excellent. When I finished the entire sales process, the nurse executive came up to me and asked, "Who will be our new CEO?" I said, "You will get some candidates from us that we'll select from a national search and from our own talent pool, and the board will make a decision on the best person, but each candidate will be fully able to do the job." She said, "I guess what I was really asking is that everybody in the hospital is saying that there's a rumor that you could be the CEO, and everyone would like you to be the CEO." I think that's kind of a quintessential example of what leadership in the sales process means to the client.

There are about four levels of leadership that occur in the sales process of an organization and one is leadership at the client level, i.e., leading the client. The second is leadership at the corporate level and on the senior management team which creates a hard and fast agreement that the marketing culture of dare will be maintained and that the marketing executives will lead that process and have absolute authority. The third level is the leadership of the sales team by the sales team leader. And the last level is the leadership of the entire corporate culture from top to bottom and from side to side with all associates that embraces the concept that every day the first thing on our minds should be where is our next client coming from.

We talked a lot about leading the client, getting into the on-site validation process and basically giving a demonstration of not only product but leadership. Product by itself is a commodity. It's the leadership that energizes it and creates the hot hope. The next step that's so important is the leadership of the sales team. Today team selling - the technical expertise of an operations person, financial person, or whatever the situation needs - is so important. It's a team, and it's easy for the senior person or the person with the greater seniority to emerge as the leader. But there can be only one quarterback.

To give an example, I was involved in a project where I was scrupulously following our process, always being aware that intelligent adaptations may be needed. You must always be listening, always aware of everything around you and all the stakeholders. In this instance, I happened to be working with the hospital board. There was an enormous schism between the board and the medical staff and, of course, bringing the medical staff into the sales process was important. The medical staff was suing the board and there was great tension between the two groups. It became very difficult to get access to all the physicians because of various logistical problems. The operations person on the project said he thought we had a real breakdown in the sales process - basically saying the sales team wasn't doing it right. I asked what is the breakdown? He said we don't have the medical staff on board and the board itself is very splintered, and the hospital itself might not be one where we can be successful. I told this person, you're right, this project is different because of some logistical foul-ups at the local level due to lack of organization, but even so, it's important that right now we realize that selling the medical staff and getting them to endorse us is the worst possible choice, because the board will do the opposite of whatever the medical staff wants. So what we would like is the approval of a few key leaders – quietly. We won't wave the fact that the medical staff supports us in the face of the board so we're going to de-emphasize that in our presentation and written report. He said he strongly disagreed and had a real problem with it and didn't think I was doing my job. I said I'm going to relieve you of all of your anxiety right now. This is my call, this is my decision and this is the call I'm making and I am totally accountable - only me - for the outcome. You are now relieved of all anxiety and responsibility and if it goes to hell in a hand basket, I will raise my hand and say it's my fault. In the meantime, either you will support me in every strategy and tactic I choose to implement, or we will replace you and remove you from the sales team. That was important. That was part of courage and that was part of dare and that was part of having confidence and knowing that you have the authority to make those decisions unequivocally and with the support of senior management.

The first thing I say to everyone is that they need to understand the importance of marketing in the company. It's not a division, it's not a department, it's not a support function and here's why. Nothing happens in any company in the United States of America or on the globe until somebody sells something first. We don't need operations people, service people, support people, or manufacturers unless the sale has been made. Otherwise we're just losing more and more money. So that is the point. It is the corporate culture that has to be communicated from the CEO level throughout the whole organization so that marketing is elevated to the appropriate position, because nobody has a job until somebody sells something and the people responsible for selling should be the experts in selling. And it's really true that, while selling is different than other business skills in that there is no major at the Harvard Business School or Wharton in selling (we have it in Business Administration, Operations and Logistics, Finance and everything else but we don't have it in selling), it's usually not viewed as an area of expertise to be learned in a very technical and methodical way. It's really something that everybody who's trained in something else figures out on the fly and kind of wings it. They read some books and attend seminars, but they never understand that selling really is a science, a discipline and a very technical area. Therefore, the marketing people, who have that expertise and have that understanding, clearly and decisively have to be empowered to be in charge of that process. And in the matrix management approach everyone effectively reports to marketing when the company is in selling mode. The marketing person, not the operations person, makes the call in the sales process when the tough ones have to be made - that's just appropriate separation of church and state. Even though it's a team, even though the company has a culture where marketing and operations work in a cyclical process, when we get to the selling part, operations must step aside so marketing can make the call.

There are two principles of the sales process that I notice that a lot of organizations miss, and they are so important. They are often missed by a lot of sales executives at all levels of the company and by people who are involved in the sales process – often because there's so much ego and so much machismo tied up in this process, e.g., "I am courageous, I am tough, and I will never quit," etc. These two principles are the hardest things to implement and require great strength, great leadership, great confidence and great empowerment. The first is to walk away. If you really just think about the probability - everything in sales is about probability - so many leads equal so many closures, and if the process is working, you can maximize the closures. So to close, you are talking about looking at your common denominators. If you have 1,000 leads in a year and you only have so many hours of man time, let's pick a number - a 1,000 hours - that's an hour per lead. Let's say you spend five hours on something that really isn't a lead at all. Now you have lost five hours pursuing five other leads which are not going to get worked appropriately to closure. What a lot of salespeople have trouble with is being willing to say, "that's not a deal and we're not going to spend one more minute on it." They're concerned that they may be criticized within the company, e.g., well, you quit too soon - what makes you so smart? - what are you doing this on, intuition or what? The answer is yes. I have excellent intuition and I trust my judgment. I'm not always right, but I'm right nine out of ten times, and I'm going to find the next five real ones and not waste any more time on this. If you really just think about the math, this is one of the killers for any company - not knowing when to say that one's over or that one's not worth starting.

The second sales principle that organizations often miss is a little different but it's a part of the selling process. This is something I learned - that especially at the critical moment in a transaction, when you've done everything and you're not quite there yet and you just don't want to do nothing, that's when sometimes it's important to recognize that doing nothing is a conscious choice. It is a tactical option, and it can often be the correct option. When you're there, you're there. If it ain't broke, don't fix it. And that takes real confidence to make the judgment. It's possibly the hardest of all calls. But when you do it and it works out, you just say to yourself thank God I didn't do anything else. It's ironic how sometimes you'll think, well, we could do XYZ thing, and the client will tell you he "wants you for all these reasons, and by the way, just so you know, your competition did this at the last minute and it really aggravated us," and it was precisely what you were going to attempt yourself. You just say, boy, did we dodge a bullet.

Something I talked about before and I want to go back to is the concept that as soon as possible in the sale process, one must have the courage and professionalism to explain an evaluative process to a client. The steps of the sales process that we recommend to the client are steps that we take together with him in order to evaluate the best approach for him. We tell him that we know there is a possibility we may not be his best alternative. We tell him that we may even realize during the process that, while our model is excellent, it might not be as effective for you or us because of the way your organization is structured. If we get to that point, we'll disengage. That gives people a comfort level up front. They know that you're really objective about helping them and not just hell-bent on making a sale. This tends to lower the resistance to going forward with the process and agreeing on a timetable. Locking that in is critically important. What it really does show to the client is that you have a lot of esteem for your company and yourself, and that you value your time, you value your resources. Frankly, it brings a dimension of privilege to the client to have you involved in their organization and for you to be willing to work with them. It sort of evens the playing field is probably a better way to say it, because it really sets the expectation that staying on that timeframe is critical. Most sales organizations ignore the opportunity to establish a timetable for closure, and what's interesting is that many times the client will ask me if that really is enough time? I go over the steps with them to make them feel more comfortable so that they will focus on the time between when they get their proposal and when you want a decision which ideally is short. But I remind them that the overall process will be as many as six to eight weeks, and I tell them that one of the important things in any business partnership (defining the term "partnership" loosely here - not as a joint venture but as a relationship) is decisiveness. We need to be very decisive about how we approach each situation and clear about the services we provide, and we need an equally decisive client. Whether its software or whatever, implementation is everything and it requires decisiveness. We say to our client that one of the reasons we structure the process in this way is because we like to work and we are successful when we work with decisive leaders. We're decisive leaders and what we've told our client is a form of testing them, because what we found is that the leaders of an organization who can come to a decision on the established time cycle have the element of leadership and strength that we would need to be successful working for them and with them. Those who cannot are clients we probably wouldn't be successful with. So in effect while you test us, this is our one test for you, and we do ask you to just tell us your decision, because we can take "no" as graciously as "yes."

The following sales concept really refers back to the subject of "no decision." The first warning sign of "no decision" is when the client has all the information necessary to make a decision and says he just needs one more thing or more time. Do a quick inventory of all the data that has been provided and ask, "What one piece of information would you need to make the decision that you don't already have?" What you get is, one of two things. He says, "You're right we have everything we need; it's the decision itself we're struggling with - just taking the plunge." Or else the person says, "I'll give you a list of the other things I need." That's what I call getting lost in the statistical blizzard, because there are no questions left. And interestingly, in one organization I worked with we said to the client that maybe it was actually the decision itself he was struggling with and his answer was, that's right. You know, what's funny is that probably as many as 50 of my clients that I can think of off the top of my head have said, "You know it's interesting, I had the greatest tension right before we made that decision and the minute we made it I had an enormous sense of relief. It's funny because it was making the decision itself that alleviated my anxiety, not pondering the decision further." It can help to alleviate their anxiety and overcome it by providing them with a complete reference list and getting them on the phone with existing clients. In this way they realize they're not the first person in the world to make a decision. So often in the sales process clients don't do the reference verification. We try to get them to use it, but there's an art to getting the client to do that, though it really gets them over those hurdles.

In the sales process the word that I like to hear most often applied to me is "focus." When somebody says this person is one of the most focused individuals I have ever met, that's a great compliment. To some people it may mean that this person is a little "unifocal," maybe he doesn't balance things well. But what that means in the sales world is that you're dealing with a competent professional who understands how to prioritize. In my mind every deal starts like the opening kick-off of a football game. You know that when you start on the five yard line and have 95 yards to go, there is a certain degree of probability, which is low, and there is a certain degree of optimism and intensity. When the salesperson gets the ball down to the opposite one yard line and has one yard to go, and he's as worried as the client about the ball on the one yard line, he must insure that he gives 100% focus on pushing it over the goal line to closure. In the sales process, the salesperson must not give equal effort to when the ball is on the 50 yard line as he does to when it's on the 10 yard line and then on the one yard line. It's not a sign of his ability to balance and juggle. It's actually a sign of incompetence. What you need to realize is that the ball on the one yard line is the one you absolutely have to put all of your energy into at that point in time and push over quickly. The key is that focus means speed. Speed means efficient sales cycle time. It means that once the ball goes into the end zone, you can then put all your attention and tenacity back on the other balls in a balanced way - with the next ball being the next closest to the goal line. It's the person who gives equal weight to the ball on the one yard line as he did on the earlier yard lines line who draws the sales cycle out and it becomes less efficient. Instead of another hour or two, it will take two weeks to get closure on that one before he can go to the next ball. I think it is most important to realize that concept (if you believe in the concept of following a sales process), because it is transferable between organizations - especially in the B-to-B world. You've seen it work, and you have to understand that it will take incredible endurance and focus on the detail. Every detail is important. A very good salesperson is more like a sprinter than a marathon runner. But the excellent salesperson is both. It's the sprint that brings closure yet it's one sprint after another, a marathon at high speed, that brings long term success.

There's a link between focus, tenacity and courage in that order. Everything starts with focus. If you believe in a process approach and you follow a process approach, it works. It might sound like a real stretch, but imagine a brain surgeon who wasn't focused and the outcome he would have. Every step is critical; every cut is critical. It's the same way with a sales process. While there are maybe five or six major steps, there also are a 1,000 little steps that the professional knows and checks off in his mind. He is focused on the steps, doing the right steps in the right order, not missing anything, and just constantly scrutinizing his deal, the status, the last communication, and what he forgot. I always think in terms of my "rule of three," i.e., what are the three things I have to make happen to get the deal and what are the three things that I have to prevent from happening to get this deal. These are all required tactical steps that must be checked out. To the extent that I have that focus, something really simple happens. I realize that I already know I am ahead of my competition because nobody can out-focus me, and that pushes up my courage.

Tenacity enters in when things don't go the way I planned them and wanted them to go. It's basically course correction time. What sometimes happens is if it looks like we really have a problem and we're not going to be successful, we have to provide the focus. If we are thinking negatively, then we are thinking the problem is the obstacle, and we're not thinking of the solution. I always like to think every lead is a deal - that it's just a matter of finding the right path, and if I find the right path and take the right steps, then every lead will be a deal. That's where tenacity comes in. Tenacity is staying in there when things aren't going right and going back to focus on the solution and the path around the obstacle. It's the focus, and if you are being tenacious, what happens is that you revisit the process, and because you know the process is effective, that feeds into your courage. Of course, then the courage you have increases your empowerment to dare. If any one piece is absent, if there's insufficient focus, then your courage goes down because you haven't done it right. It weakens your confidence and, frankly, if you missed a step, you look to your client like you don't know what you're talking about, and you know that too. But if you cover every base, if the rationale for your sale is tight, and if you've pulled all the emotional triggers, you know you're in a position to close. If you've done it all right, not only do you recognize that but your client recognizes that as well. When you close he says, yeah, it does make sense because you've covered all your bases.

Price is always a key issue in closure and it's very interesting. It's my general observation that there is a pricing methodology, a negotiating methodology which is universally accepted and used in America which is: if I expect you to pay me $1, then I'll tell you the price is $1.50 and you will say I had in mind $.50 and we'll negotiate on $1. I guess that approach works, it does for a lot of people. But there's another approach that works better. If you really believe that you provide the best service or product, then it should be priced at a premium because, even at a premium price, it is the best value to your client. Another approach which I've employed uses the dare and courage factor. It is a practical approach that you must use very carefully. This is when you present your fee and you set expectations in advance and you remind the client of the value you're already adding in the sales process - you're doing the ROI measurement. You're spending your professional's time and money to come be their staff for a week. If you do it correctly, in advance, you say, "When I present you with a fee, I will present you with one fee for your consideration. We can take a yes or a no (obviously a no less graciously than a yes), but that will be the fee, and it will represent the best combination of fee and service to equal maximum value, so we'll ask you for a decision on that." We may present them with two options on the fee that are tied to the term of the contract. When people come to me and say, "This is good but what about the fee?" what they are really saying to you is that you've done it right and you've shown an ROI, and they've already emotionally made the buy. And if you've done it right and followed the process, and if they're 100% sold, then there's no need to negotiate any fee. What I like to do is personalize things.

I've always found there are basically two schools of thought on fee. One is the $1.50, .50, okay, we'll call it a buck approach which to me is not an ethical approach. The ethical approach is to say, we know what our costs are, we know what your return is going to be, and we know what is a reasonable profit for our company, and what we've done is taken the high, ethical approach and given you the best number right up front. The client has the best number available and now all we need from him is a decision on it. Our best number has been established in the context of the product, because what we've said is that we've measured carefully and together with all of your stakeholders, through an extensive process, have carefully defined your goals. We've measured what services and what costs are needed to get to their goals. An unacceptable school of thought regarding fees is to diminish the package of services that are necessary to achieve the client's goal. We would know in our heart-of-hearts that they will not be successful, we will not be successful, and we will all be disappointed. Can you really imagine yourself in the position of getting to this point and the client doesn't feel that there is sufficient return to justify the fee? Can you really imagine that? I don't think so. The other thing I like to do is make a statement to the client that this is not a corporate philosophy, this is my personal philosophy. There's a way to deal with a client's concern about their fee. Frankly, this is just my view on how you conduct business professionally and ethically at all times. I am very honest with the client up front. I tell them I will give them one, maybe two, pricing options, and then ask them to select, and when I do, I'm doing what I said I would do. I think in terms of justifying the fee, the focus is always on benefits. I tell them, "These are your goals, imagine that your current discomfort, your organizational pain or turmoil, is all eliminated, your return is here, morale is high and all you've paid is this fee. If you see yourself in that position, I think you probably agree that the fee is basically insignificant right where it is."

One of the amazing things I've noticed when I think about the leadership aspect of a whole sales group, or I talk about the senior leader of the marketing/sales function in a company, is that by their nature, salespeople tend to be good guys, gregarious, get-along with everybody. They all have a good sense of humor and they like to stay loose. Most sales leaders are cut from that cloth. Their careers started in a sales executive role and they moved up the chain of command. You find a lot of sales managers who are concerned about maintaining that good guy image and keeping it fun, because they know the extreme pressure their people are under at all times and they really need to help them ventilate. But what really works best is a lot of toughness from the sales leader executive. It's really a balance, an interesting balance.

One of the most important things sales leaders do for their salespeople is to help them recognize the fact that the best time to make a sale is about one second after they have just made a sale, because their confidence is high. I think most salespeople's (even the best) normal instincts after closing a transaction is basically to go into a self-congratulatory mode and take the next day or two – the two best days to go make the next sale - and waste it celebrating, congratulating and calming down from the whole intense sales experience. In reality, the organizations that focus on the fact that right after a sale is the best time to make the next sale - that keep their people focused - are probably the most successful. People who sustain long careers in sales learn this early on. Something I find that works best for a loss of a sale is actually a formal, allowable mourning period. For me it's always been three days; I'll give myself three days. I also recognized that three days was too long so I learned to shorten it to half a day and keep it there. For the worst tragic loss in history, I'll allow myself to feel bad for three days while I still function, but I will not allow myself to feel bad anymore after that. Even then, I try to shorten it to half a day. I think for organizations that actually have a defined, acceptable and allowable mourning period (and we all kind of mourn together) that the one day rule is the best. These organizations are the most successful.

Also, the post-mortem is important. Many organizations simply say, well, we lost it. That creates bogeymen. In your own mind, you have all kinds of horrible thoughts as to why you lost it and that can completely erode your confidence. If you go back to the client and ask why you lost, my experience is there is always one or two very specific reasons and usually you get down to issues that are never scary. There may be a relationship factor involved or something like that. More importantly, you may have missed a step in the process. But as important, you are creating the discipline to go back and see if you implemented the process correctly. If you did, what you discover is that you were beaten because of a relationship factor or some uncontrollable variable that all the power in heaven and earth could not have changed, and that is easy to accept. What is difficult to accept for anybody who is truly successful, is when they made a mistake and they could have had the deal. Going through that process creates the rigor and discipline to simply not let that happen again.

Since most selling today is group selling, what's amazing to me is how one can get so focused on a particular decision maker, even if it's the top decision maker or some key influence. Often we focus solely on one or two people when there are, in fact, a lot of stakeholders involved in the sales process. Once, when trying to complete a transaction, we realized clearly that we had lost. The decision wasn't finalized, yet we knew we had lost, so we thought about it and knew we still had a day or two to come up with a miracle. We had an idea. I said, "If we know we are going to lose the game, let's change the game." What we did was to go back and radically restructure the entire transaction and give the client something they didn't even think of which totally changed the ground rules and saved the deal. Group sales are pretty interesting because, for instance, if you're selling to an organization that is important to a community and your key leadership or the board are not on board with what's happening, you're free to increase the number of stakeholders involved in the decision and control that part of the process. In other words, the key decision maker can come from the informal organization. You can convert that person from an "A" decision maker to a "B" decision maker and basically get a bigger dog. We did that in Lebanon, Missouri when we were short one vote on a board. I realized this community had created a tremendous industrial base with Emerson Electronics Plant, a state-of-the-art, brand new, $250 million business which was building a second plant. They were the only industry in town. It occurred to me that I'm sure a vote by this board involving the hospital in this community has got to be pretty important to Emerson. So we visited Emerson and asked them about the hospital, what could be better, and they gave us some ideas. Then we thought about who created this industrial base in this small burg in the middle of Missouri and the answer was the mayor. He'd been mayor for 30 years. We visited the mayor and said to him this is who we are and what we are doing and asked what do you think about that? Then we asked, how do you think the hospital is doing and he said, it's doing okay. We said, you have an airstrip here that's a mile long and can handle jet aircraft - this is a highly advanced community. How would you feel if the hospital doesn't do well in the future and maybe closes? He said that would be a tragedy and could undermine our whole industrial base. And we said, we'll just offer you this thought: we're short one vote on your board and they are going to make a decision tonight. The vote became unanimous with the mayor's input. He was a fabulous leader, a visionary, and he followed through and got it all done. So by looking at all the stakeholders involved and realizing that, although it's usually ideal to minimize the number of decision makers and participants in the sales process on the client's end, sometimes it is an advantage to expand the number of people involved in the decision. Because, if you have a person that's an intractable "no" and who is the key decision maker, increasing the number of stakeholders is the only solution.

One more thought on this. Apply this principle to other industries. For instance, if you sell XYZ microchips to Dell Computers, and they sell the computers to large corporate clients, and you're making your presentation to the computer company who's going to buy your microchips, one approach is to go to THEIR customer and leapfrog YOUR customer and extract knowledge from their customer about what's important to them (delivery time, turnaround time, dependability), and then come back and say, your biggest client said XYZ microchips are the most important to us when we buy Dell computers.

On the subject of the "no" votes in the sales process, there are usually one or two people that I call the intractable no, and human nature says, well let me play the math here. If there are ten decision makers involved and one ultimate decision maker, and if it is pretty much a consensus-driven process, who owns the math is in my favor. If I win five to four, that's as good as nine-0 but, in reality, it's critically important to be with the intractable no. Why? The first reason is that it shows disrespect to leave them out and not show them the same attention and courtesy. If they're agitated or just don't care for you or your product, it makes things worse. The second reason, in my experience, is that converting an intractable no to a yes is a pretty rare event. That's because the person usually has deep-seated emotional reasons and no logical reasons to hold onto their position, and that's very difficult to overcome. It can be done, but the thing that is critical is to gather intelligence about that person's mindset from other people before sitting down with that individual. Part of being intractable means not being open and not sharing information in most cases. If there's some history you need to know about the person's mindset, background or past experience, you're going to have to get it from another source. Then you must illicit those issues by asking questions that are right on point. If you can do that, you have a place to start to break down the emotional problems and issues.

One example comes to mind in working with a board member who was an intractable no. He was a school teacher. He said his problem was that he knew of two organizations to which we had provided services and left, and that those organizations had not done that well with our product and services. I knew this man was a school teacher, so I said, I understand that and I guess what you're saying is there is probably nothing I can say to you that will make you change your mind. Even calling our positive references which are overwhelming compared to the few organizations where things just didn't work out. And he said, you're right, you'll never convince me of this. I respect you and your company, but I just really feel strongly. Then I said, what else do you want to talk about and he said, I don't care. I said, we're not finished with lunch after all. I asked, when did you retire? And he told me, a few years ago. Although I knew he was a school teacher, I asked, what did you do? And he said, I was a school teacher. I asked, how is education going in these parts these days? And he said, good, we have a good system in place. I asked, how are SAT scores in Texas, and he said, they're moving up, it's a bell curve. I said, it's a bell curve, really? And he said, yeah. And I asked, when you were a teacher, just curious, how did people tend to grade out? What did you have, about 20 kids in the class? And he said, right around 20. And I asked, what percentage of A's, B's, C's? And he said, at least 4 A's, a lot of B's and C's, and about 4-5 D's, and one F. And I said, so in other words, you took all your resources and attention and gave it to the kids with the A's and B's. And to the C's you said, I'll give you a little attention, and to the D's you said, why don't you sit at the very back of the class? I don't have much time for you. And to the kid with the F you said, why don't you stand out in the hall because I don't have enough time and resources to help you out? And he said, of course not. I gave every student the same attention and care. And I asked, what went wrong? And he said, sometimes the students just didn't want to try. And I said, remember when we were talking about those two hospitals down the road where it didn't work out? I said, these are business relationships that involved literally hundreds of stakeholders, physicians, employees, community. Marriage is a relationship and it only involves two parties and there is a divorce rate of nearly 50%. And he said, I get your point, and I can't believe it but I'm willing to call your references to see what you can do when it works. He ultimately voted positive.

The absolute intractable no. That's an example of winning one. More commonly, what you're going to have to do is move somebody who's really negative. Hopefully, at a minimum, if they're hostile and damaging, you move them from that position to a neutral position. It can often be done. Generally, if there is really an intractable no, they probably have a misconception and bad information. It's critically important, in a non-offensive way, to get to the root of the problem and the misconception. If you can do it and follow up and prove to them with something concrete that they're wrong, what they inevitably will do is move to a role of quietness and neutrality and probably embarrassment, because they were spreading incorrect information about you and your product/service to other stakeholders and decision makers, and you proved to them they were incorrect. Then they no longer have a reason to remain negative, but because they were so intractably negative previously, they feel that out of ego they can't change their position. At least they will be quiet, because they don't want you to prove to the entire world that what they said was grossly inaccurate. This happened to us in a hospital in New Jersey when we presented a candidate for the CEO position in a management contract. A board member called a former executive at a health system where our candidate was an executive director to validate that she had worked there and had, in fact, held the position of executive director. The former executive said no, she was VP of something, but she was never executive director. But he was simply wrong. He had already left the organization before our candidate moved up to executive director and held it for three years managing $200 million of operations. The board member came back and told the entire board that she had a hole in her resume and that we had misrepresented her credentials. He caused an enormous stir. When we came back and said it IS valid and told them the name of the current CEO and that she reported to him directly, the board member was very embarrassed and quickly went into the background. Unfortunately, he did a lot of damage that was not reparable.

One of the most important things to remember is that whatever you're selling is a commodity. Thus, no matter how great you believe your technical advantage is or your differential advantage versus competition, you are still selling a commodity. When you really think about it, price is a function of doing a good job of selling, and there is generally a lot of price elasticity with clients. The cowardly salesperson likes to think there isn't power in stretching the fee. The courageous person thinks there is power because it's all about value, and he is good at presenting value.

Another very important thing to always remember is that emotions are key to the deal. I've always found that early on in the sales process, especially when working with a decision maker or someone who has key influence, if you can win trust in a very personal way, there is nothing more powerful. To form a relationship that goes beyond the minute, there is nothing like it. I like to take the high risk approach. I like to make the fact real clear to someone up front and convince them it's true, i.e., if I don't think we're a good fit for the situation or in any way not the best, we'll walk away.

I always think in sales that people buy on emotion first, people buy from people second, and third, closure is everything. I think most salespeople recognize that they're selected because they are likable people, they're personable, etc. But what they can lose sight of is that it's important to make a first impression and part of that is small talk - you know we chat about the golf pictures, the pictures of the kids. We wear our best suits and all those good things. The better salesperson looks beyond first impressions and focuses on building the person-to-person relationship from start to finish. No matter how good it starts, you would hope to be a factor of ten better as you get to closure. That's the other point. I think you do that by focusing on how the sale of the service or product is going to affect that human being and their company. How it makes their life better. How it reduces pain.

V. SALES PHILOSOPHY AND PROCESS

All Corporate Functions and the Operational Sales Force as Salesdriven

There must be a philosophy within an organization which encourages an overlap or interdependence between operations and sales. In order to be successful, these functions can never really be viewed as two distinct functions. The whole culture of the company must be marketing driven. The important ingredients of success are significant delegation and team building. There is no conflict between operations and sales when operations people feel they are part of the process.

Internally, there must be a strong sales presence at the senior management level, i.e., founder of company, president or chief operating officer. Additionally, centralization/control of the entire sales/marketing process is important where sales is "Captain of the Ship" from lead generation to collection of the check. This is where the whole philosophy of the company is marketing driven.

Marketing and operations are overlapping functions; thus, a marketing department should not be a separate division of the company, but instead an organizational overlay so that marketing becomes a culture that drives a company.

As a result of the above, a company, through its own employees and existing clients, could generate nearly all its future sales opportunities. This requires spending considerable time educating both the employees of a company as well as existing clients on the benefits of growing the organization. For the clients, the economies of scale achieved by the company through growth is ultimately to their benefit.

The Process of Selling

The decision making process is a common path to a common goal for the sales executive and the customer thereby reducing variance in the behaviors of the marketing/sales executive and the client. This creates an atmosphere for the development of a productive relationship with the client through a sense of purpose, conviction, strength, and thus leadership.

The Sales Process is specifically designed to build confidence and courage in the Sales/Operations team and more important, set their expectations for success which, by the way, is subliminally transferred to the prospective client. In order for successful marketing to take place, the team members (Sales and Operations) must not operate from a framework of fear; accordingly, the sales process eliminates fear/panic selling. This sales process is enhanced by the utilization of statistical variance in order to look in a scientific way at marketing results and improve the "frequency of closure."

By utilizing a total quality improvement approach and a formalized understanding of the SALES PROCESS; it allows transportability of the PROCESS to most organizations irrespective of the item/service being sold. THUS, SELLING IS SELLING!!

The PROCESS must follow these simple fundamental principles:

A. Marketing must become a culture which drives a company with operations as an overlapping function.

B. Value must determine marketing success with an entrepreneurial approach.

C. Centralization and control of the marketing function and the decision making PROCESS.

Preconditions to moving ahead with the PROCESS:

A. Closure as a precondition to receiving value-added selling, to include advance scheduling of a firm decision date, makes sense since closure is the client's goal even more than it is ours. It's amazing that closure, arguably the most important step in the marketing/selling process, is often where individuals and organizations also fail. Courage and the recognition that closure is everyone's goal overcome this tendency.

B. The marketing "fence" – we have always required exclusivity as a precondition to accessing our professional consultative analysis at no monetary cost.

C. Agreement to conduct diligent on-site research – In selling, we must always keep in mind that the process is often a process of discovery, especially with regard to the marketing, selling of services.

D. Due diligence by the client – In advance of agreeing to enter into the selling process, we have always made it a precondition that the client directly verify our performance and service with our existing clients.

E. Proposal presentation/closure – So, in essence, the on-site process IS the selling and proposal phase and the actual proposal presentation then becomes the forum to affect CLOSURE on or before the pre-agreed date.

VI. ACCEPTANCE SPEECH FOR PHILIP KOTLER AWARD FOR EXCELLENCE IN HEALTHCARE MARKETING

Presented at a luncheon in connection with the 16th Annual Symposium on Healthcare Marketing, Saturday, June 15, 1996, 12:00 Noon at Sheraton Boston Hotel and Towers, Boston, Massachusetts; Sponsored by the Healthcare Marketing Division of the American Marketing Association

As you heard in the introduction, my background is that of a trained hospital administrator and entrepreneur, therefore, I am honored and humbled because midway in my career I have tried to become a marketing-oriented business executive. I am especially honored because all of you are professionally trained people who have spent a good part of your life entirely as marketing executives. I came into this "arena" late, from operations, because I saw an overlap or interdependence of operations and marketing and never really viewed them as two distinct functions. With this in mind, I co-founded three marketing-driven healthcare companies, including a hospital management company, a diabetes treatment management company and a PPO management company for rural area. I also view the "world" from the perspective of marketing fairly customized healthcare services to organizations, mainly hospitals, where the universe of potential clients is relatively finite. As you probably notice, working within this relatively small universe has allowed me to take liberty with how I define an approach of the marketing function. For these reasons, the terms "marketing" and "selling" have always been interchangeable.

The people I've admired most throughout my career seem to always keep two things in mind. First...*the customer comes first*. That is to say, the first obligation of anyone in business is to be certain their products or services truly help the customer achieve something desirable. For patients, this means improved health or quality of life at less cost; for physicians, perhaps simplification of the rigors of private practice or, for organizations (such as a hospital), the attainment of important patient care or financial goals. If these things occur, then we pursue business on the highest ethical and moral ground, and we can therefore do so with the greatest enthusiasm and self respect possible. And, profits will then be simply the natural by-product of all of this.

Second...the revenue generation begins precisely at the moment of closure of a sale. All activities which precede the closure of a sale are measured in terms of their cost, or to put it another way, from an entrepreneur's perspective, nothing happens until somebody sells something. As a result, the aspect of marketing which I have come to value most is the *sales* aspect. That point where each of our companies or organizations actually touches the customer intellectually, emotionally, and through a handshake, even physically.

Please don't misunderstand me! Data is crucial. Market research points us to potential customers and enables us to define their needs. However, at some point we need to change gears so that our focus shifts from facts, statistics and product attributes to a focus on a particular "human" and his or her "customer" needs. There is a risk to relying on data, at least in the final phase of the marketing process, i.e., the sales process, and that is that the process can bog down in a statistical blizzard and become impersonal.

Ultimately, we sell goods and services to people and we know that people buy from people.

Since there will always be at least one competitor whose product or service is nearly identical . . . or at least once price is factored into the equation, of equal *value* . . . then, ultimately, we come back to the fundamental reality that:

> *People buy from people.*
> *People buy on emotion.*
> *People buy when the sale is closed by a professional.*

All things being equal, people will always do business with a friend. In fact, my 30 years of professional experience have taught me . . . all things being not quite so equal, people will still do business with a friend. From my experience, I know that people respond to the phrase, "All things being not quite so equal." It has lots of resonance about the importance of building and maintaining relationships.

RELATIONSHIPS

I. Relationships/Lead Generation

In a perfect world, lead generation would be self-perpetuating. That means that a company, through its own employees and existing clients, would generate all the leads necessary to generate future sales opportunities. This is the model that we have tried to achieve over the years; whereas, we have actually spent only a small fraction of our marketing dollars on traditional advertising modalities. We have instead spent considerable time educating both our employees (associates) and existing clients on the benefits of growing our organization. For our clients, the economies of scale achieved by our company through growth is ultimately to their benefit. We impart this knowledge to our customers both informally and formally through various educational programs. As a result, over the last several years, our company has generated 85% of its leads internally; that is through employees of the company or existing clients.

II. Relationships/Making the Sale

There is transportability of the marketing PROCESS within healthcare as well as to non-healthcare service organizations. Healthcare, of course, is different because of its service nature, life or death situations, physician relationships and difficult quality of care evaluation concerns; thus, I am convinced of the transportability of the PROCESS within healthcare and, with limitations, to non-healthcare organizations given the uniqueness of our business. A few fundamental principles have guided my thinking about organizations, their goals, and marketing's relationship to all of this.

A. *Marketing and Operations are overlapping functions; thus, a marketing department should not be a separate division of the company but instead an organizational overlay, so that marketing becomes a culture that drives a company.*

B. *The entrepreneurial nature of marketing is demonstrated when value determines marketing success. In our case, the number of successful contracts in hospitals throughout the nation.*

C. *Centralization is the importance of controlling the marketing function from the initial call to the collection of the check. Marketing is "Captain of the Ship."*

MARKETING PROCESS

In the early 90s, Quorum utilized Dr. Deming's teachings on quality and introduced a major division of the company called the Center for Continuous Improvement (CCI) - a formalized understanding of a marketing PROCESS which I had used in other settings, and we were later able to formalize it, i.e., the use of total quality improvement in the marketing PROCESS and accordingly:

A. *The utilization of statistical variance to be able to look in a scientific way at marketing results, i.e., periodic market track reports which analyze targeting activities, lead generation, selling opportunities and frequency of closure. We also used many other sophisticated mechanisms to look at variance.*

B. *This marketing process is specifically designed to build confidence and courage in the marketing/operations team and, more importantly, set their expectations for success, which by the way, I believe is subliminally transferred to the client, i.e., our clients often ask us our conversion rate and when they learn it's 80%, they expect to do business with us. In order for successful marketing to take place, the team members (marketing and operations) must not operate from a framework of FEAR, and the marketing process eliminates fear/panic marketing.*

Centralization/control of marketing PROCESS with strong marketing presence is necessary at senior management level, i.e., founder of company or executive vice president; thus there is no conflict with operations given senior vision by company. The important ingredient to success is significant delegation and team building. In all our healthcare companies, we have moved the regional operations people closer to the client in order to have meaningful proactive marketing success. We don't have the typical conflicts between operations and marketing, because we have made the operations people feel they are part of the marketing process and not separate. This is where the whole philosophy of the company is marketing driven.

The decision making PROCESS (a common path to a common goal for the marketing executive and the customer) results in reducing variance in the behaviors for the marketing/sales executive and the client as well as creating an atmosphere for the development of a productive relationship with the client through a sense of purpose, conviction, and strength (leadership). Externally, relationship building with the client should be the guiding principle in the marketing/selling process. The creation of trust, good feelings, and the verification of a responsive detail-oriented marketing/selling professional always precedes a sale.

PRECONDITIONS TO MOVING AHEAD WITH THE PROCESS

I. Closure As A Precondition to Receiving Value-Added Selling

This includes advanced scheduling of a firm decision date which makes sense since closure is the client's goal even more than it is ours. After all, the client is trying to run a business and is working under time pressure as we all are. Their goals are time sensitive and they want to do their job. Since our organization has constantly participated in the evaluative process with other clients for years, who better to offer examples and advice on how to bring order, efficiency, and integrity to the process. It's amazing that closure, arguably the most important step in the marketing/selling process, is where individuals and organizations often fail. Courage and the recognition that closure is everyone's goal overcome this tendency.

II. The Marketing Fence

We have always required exclusivity as a precondition to accessing our professional consultative analysis at no monetary cost. Practically speaking, the way we conduct on-site research on the client's needs is so intense for all participants that it would be practically and logistically impossible for the client to repeat the process with a competitor. In essence, we use expertise as a loss leader to affect initiation and closure of the sales process.

III. Agreement to Conduct Diligent On-Site Research

In selling, we must always keep in mind that the process is often a process of discovery, especially with regard to the marketing/selling of services (i.e., because services can often be customized with relative ease). In other words, during the sales process the customer more fully explores their needs and those of their organization. Therefore, they may end up at a much different point in terms of product needs, expectations, and budget at the time of purchase versus the time of the initiation of the sales encounter. By developing a relationship we become a valuable participant in that process. We can truly offer the customer a value before the sale by providing our expertise during the consultative or evaluative process. As I said, my companies have always spent the lion's share of their marketing dollars assisting the client in this way. (Much more so than on media advertising or conventions/booths.)

Statistics can be deceiving, whereas by building relationships, communication comes naturally and enables us to truly understand the customer's needs because we asked them. That's real time or just-in-time primary market research. It can't be beaten.

Blind responses to RFP's are like buying lottery tickets . . . we just don't do it. Neither do we send our proposals over the telephone. Heck, we not only get in front of people, we move in for a week.

Yet from time to time, our work must and does conclude by letting the client know fairly that we may not be the best option in the market for their needs at a particular moment in time (for example, any hospital where HMP/Quorum "walked," i.e., Sioux Center, Iowa). We look at those occasions not as failures in selling but as successes in building our credibility.

IV. Due Diligence by the Client

In advance of agreeing to enter into the selling process, we have always made it a precondition that the client directly verify our performance and service with our existing clients. Since we always sell from the perspective of return on investment *not* price, the fact that our prospective clients will directly validate our track record for achieving a projected ROI with our exiting clients, the price objection is removed, and really every other objection is removed along with it as an obstacle to closure. Because verification that we are who we say we are is the bottom line. And most importantly, it is this due diligence which, when approached as a precondition, eliminates losses to the number one competition – No Decision.

V. Proposal Presentation/Closure

Now much of what I've just discussed may sound straightforward, but to give you an idea of the magnitude and intensity with which we have approached this, it would be the norm for our marketing executive to interview 75 to 100 members of an organization, organizations with which they work intimately, and their customers prior to presenting our final proposal. And let me tell you, the proposal at that point becomes a formality, because our client has directly observed an organization and team of professionals working harder and more diligently to help them solve their problems and gain competitive advantages - before our company has been paid a nickel than they have ever seen before. So, in essence, the on-site process *is* the selling and proposal phase, and the actual proposal presentation then becomes the forum to affect closure on or before the pre-agreed date.

In conclusion, I sum up revenue generation this way – the ability to sell is the world's single most beneficial skill - no exceptions. If you find two people in the same profession, and one is more successful than the other, then you will inevitably find that the differentiating factor between the two is salesmanship ... no exceptions.

VII. PERSONAL VIEWS OF LEADERSHIP

SHELDON L. KRIZELMAN'S PERSONAL VIEWS OF LEADERSHIP AS PRESENTED TO THE EXECUTIVE MBA PROGRAM, OWEN GRADUATE SCHOOL OF MANAGEMENT, VANDERBILT UNIVERSITY, MAY 20, 1994

I will try to describe in my comments to you today my personal view of leadership as viewed through four different eras of my career. In fact, leadership varies significantly, in my view, based on the business environment. I will list Leadership Tools and categorize them by each of the Leadership Era's as follows:

LEADERSHIP ERA I (Non-Profit Hospital Environment)

This era represents my personal view of leadership spanning multiple positions in large, non-profit teaching hospitals as CEO, COO, e.g., University Hospital, University of Kansas or St. Luke's Hospital, Cleveland, Ohio. Clearly, this non-profit business environment, along with my career as a hospital administrator, requires unique leadership qualities.

LEADERSHIP TOOLS - ERA I

Resourcefulness

Ability to Inspire

Trust

Influence Skills

Stewardship

LEADERSHIP ERA II *(Non-Profit/For-Profit Environment)*

In this era, I set forth the leadership tools required by a for-profit company to manage non-profit hospitals in either a solo role with Hospital Affiliates International, e.g., CEO of Santa Clara Valley Medical Center, affiliated with Stanford University School of Medicine, or multiple facility manager's role with HAI responsible for 20 rural and sole provider hospitals. Thus, leadership requires the balance of a for-profit company managing the assets and resources of non-profit in either a solo role under a management company or as a district manager responsible for multiple facilities.

LEADERSHIP TOOLS - ERA II

Matrix Management

Take the Heat-Distribute Rewards

Communication Skills

Flexibility

LEADERSHIP ERA III *(Entrepreneurial Environment)*

Built a company into the second largest manager of hospital beds in the nation, thus, utilizing the entrepreneurial leadership tools to build a business which managed the assets of other owners.

Additionally, founded a diabetes management company which delivered contract management of solo units in major urban hospitals dedicated to centers of excellence relative to the treatment of diabetes. Clearly, this was an entrepreneurial venture which required the leadership skills necessary to build a business and manage it with business units in primarily large urban non-profit teaching hospitals.

Finally, from an entrepreneurial viewpoint, founded a for-profit company dedicated to the management of PPOs (Preferred Provider Organization) in non-urban environments. Again, the leadership skills required to build and operate a highly entrepreneurial company that primarily related to business activities in non-profit regional medical centers in non-urban environments.

In summary, sold the PPO management company to its senior management, sold the diabetes management company to a New York Stock Exchange company, and merged the hospital management company with the leader in the industry.

LEADERSHIP TOOLS - ERA III

Risk Taking

Whatever It Takes

Results Orientation

Vision

Innovation

LEADERSHIP ERA IV *(Large Corporate Environment)*

For the past two years (1994)*, I have been in the role of Executive Vice President of the largest hospital management company in the world with 10,000 employees and sales of approximately $800 million. This leadership role in a large, highly innovative, high-growth corporation is substantially different from the previous three eras and has many unique characteristics.

LEADERSHIP TOOLS - ERA IV

Value Diversity

Teamwork

Hiring Tale

Talented People

Balance

Empowerment

Change Management

Invite Dissent

In conclusion, my career has allowed me to participate in four different eras of leadership. Accordingly, my personal view of leadership has varied dramatically as I have transitioned within these four leadership eras.

---

* *Subsequently, this company became a publicly traded company, with sales of approximately $2 billion, with 20,000 employees, at the time of my departure in 1999.*

VIII. THE "STORIES"

SEEING THE DRAMA
THAT OTHER PEOPLE MISS
&
SELLING HOT HOPE

STORY #1

In 1985 HMP worked on a project to manage the Delta Medical Center in Greenville, Mississippi. This was a 283-bed hospital which also served as the burn center for the entire state of Mississippi. This was a real opportunity for HMP to move into the big leagues. The company had been founded in 1981 so this would have been the first really big step. In this competition we went against Hospital Corporation of America (HCA) and their marketing individual was Dick Rupert. So we were really competing against HCA and, always, the concept of contract management, which we were always selling first, and then trying to sell our company second. Greenville is a city in the delta region of Mississippi which looks like it's from the 1800's. The hospital board had been in place many, many years and we had worked on this project for approximately six months and seemed to be gaining the good will of most members of the board. As part of our process we would always do a no-cost no-obligation operational survey of the hospital and interview all the board members. We could tell from our interviews that things were going very well and, of course, the interview process was really an opportunity to market our company, HMP.

One key member of the board was a man by the name of Paul Love. During the process he invited us to his house and shared all his Civil War memorabilia with us because many members of his family had played significant roles in the fighting for the South. The most memorable interview during the survey process was the one I conducted with Paul Love. Early in the interview he asked me, "What is you?" and I said, "What do you mean?" He repeated again, "What is you?" and I said, "I am not sure I know what you mean." He said, "Let me ask it again, "What is you?" and I answered, "I am an American." He said, "Maybe you do not understand. Let me ask it again. I want to know what you is?" I could see he wanted to know if I was Jewish, so I answered, "Italian." A kind of smile came over his face and we went on with the interview, and eventually we ended up winning this major contract against HCA.

A little after the contract was signed I hired Dick Rupert, the marketing individual for HCA, to join HMP as a member of our marketing staff because I was impressed with him. Early on he asked me, "Shelly, do you remember that Paul Love down in Greenville, Mississippi where HCA lost the contract to you and HMP?" I said, "How could you forget Mr. Love?" He said, "You know I called him afterwards to kind of do an audit of the process and see where we fell down, and he said, 'Well, the main thing was that that Shelly Krizelman was one great marketing guy, and you know, Rupert, that boy is Italian. You know I thought he might be a Jew, but he said he is Italian and I liked him so I voted for him.'" Anyway, just another experience and another day in marketing. It ended up being one of the most successful contracts in the history of HMP, and it could have had a different outcome depending on how I had answered that key question during the interview process. I knew we would never change Mr. Love's prejudices and we needed to keep our eye on getting this important contract and the related revenue.

STORY #2

The next story involves the marketing of Edward Hospital in Naperville, Illinois. This was a very important project. It was a 187-bed hospital in a suburb of Chicago that would finally put HMP on the map. It was our first significant hospital beyond those that we acquired through our previous days at Hospital Affiliates International (HAI), and it was a much sought-after hospital by many large hospital systems in the Chicago area. Of course in those early days (this is 1982) we were not flying to market our accounts but driving a 1980 Olds '98 diesel which in the end, by the way, had over 200,000 miles on it.

We had driven to a wedding in Superior, Wisconsin from Nashville (that is Bob Huseby, myself, and Tom Singleton) and made a marketing visit on the way up in Naperville, Illinois. On the way back we stopped in Naperville to make a critical second visit. We went out to dinner to continue our marketing with the Chairman of the Board, a business executive in the Chicago area, and a man by the name of Dwayne Carlson, Chairman of the Search Committee and also the national president of Blue Cross. They suggested that we go to this French restaurant. Of course we did and, of course, we had no money; we were just starting our company. The first thing that Dwayne and the Chairman of the Board did was order very expensive fancy French wine which absolutely floored us. Well, the dinner proceeded nicely, and as we started with an appetizer, Bob Huseby and I were very intensely presenting the position of HMP. Meanwhile, Tom Singleton, known as a voracious eater, was enjoying French onion soup rather than being engaged in the conversation. Early in our discussion, while Bobby Huseby and myself were focused on the Chairman of the Board and the Chairman of the Search Committee, I could see out of the corner of my eye that Tom had spilled French onion soup over the front of his white shirt and tie. Rather than stop - it was a very critical point in our marketing - I just kept talking until finally the Chairman of the Search Committee, Dwayne Carlson, looked at me and started laughing. He said "Don't you think we ought to stop and see if Tom is injured and has any burns on his chest and clean up his tie and shirt?"

The point behind all of this is that when we were making marketing presentations, there was nothing, nothing in the world, that could interrupt our presentation - including scalding French onion soup down the front of one of our colleagues. We did get this major account. This story describes the intensity and focus of the marketing process during which nothing could or should interrupt an important sales point.

STORY #3

The next story revolves around the signing of Opelousas General Hospital in Opelousas, Louisiana. This is a 250-bed hospital in the heart of Cajun country about an hour and a half west of Baton Rouge and about 45 minutes North of Lafayette, Louisiana. The CEO of the hospital was Daryl Wagley and the Chairman of the Board was Sidney Sandoz, a man who is about 80 years old and had been Chairman of the Board for the past 50 years. He had a general store in Opelousas which was kind of a landmark. (This was the second hospital that we signed in July of 1981 and a very important one.) The hospital was previously managed by Hospital Affiliates International (HAI) and as a former senior officer there, I had developed a wonderful working relationship, and they wanted to continue with the same people that they had been involved with. We stayed in a renovated area of the hospital because we could not afford a hotel room and, of course, as was our custom, we drove to Opelousas in our diesel Oldsmobile - a 12 to 13 hour drive - to make a proposal to the board for the management of the hospital.

After the drive from Nashville, we waited for our presentation that evening in our auto which we parked in a city park in Opelousas along with bums and other local characters. We changed clothes in the auto for our later presentation. We had formed HMP on July 1, so this was just a few days later. After making the presentation to the board, we of course had with us a draft copy of a contract - a multi year contract of several hundred thousand dollars. The board, after hearing our presentation, decided right on the spot to enter into an agreement with us. After the meeting I went up to Mr. Sandoz, the COB, and said that I had a proposed copy of the contract that he, the board and their chief legal counsel could review and make any comments, corrections or suggestions on and then, over the next few weeks, we would finalize the agreement. Mr. Sandoz, in his great Cajun style where your word is everything and handshake is everything said, "Shelly, does it say what you says it says?" I said, "Yeah, Mr. Sandoz," and thought for a minute and realized what an awesome responsibility that was. He said, "Well, just give me the contract and I am going to sign right now on behalf of the board and the Hospital Authority and execute it to begin effective immediately." I said, "Well don't you want the other members of the board and your legal counsel to do an intensive review, which is customary?" He said, "I'll ask you again, does it say what you says is says?" And I thought for a moment again, and answered "Yes." He said, "Give me the contract and I am going to sign it."

I never had an experience quite like that - no legal counsel present on behalf of the client. I took that responsibility at Opelousas to be an awesome responsibility. I treated it so seriously because of the word and the handshake being everything. He was putting his enormous faith in me and the other principals of the company and not in a written contract. It was very characteristic of the style in Cajun country and very reflective of a Cajun-wise businessman who had led the board to great success over 50 years. Over the many years of this contract I considered it the most important contract because I had this unbelievable moral obligation to fulfill with Mr. Sandoz.

STORY #4

The next story relates to Phelps County Medical Center in Rolla, Missouri. This is a large hospital which is the sole provider in this community of 50,000 in which there is also the University of Missouri at Rolla. This is a 258-bed hospital where we signed a multi year big management agreement in 1985. The Chairman of the Board at this hospital was a man named Don Castleman who was also president of the major bank in town. He was also the predominant player in terms of bringing in HMP. This was a very hard-fought battle over many months to win this management agreement.

One of the most interesting stories was related to a meeting with Don Castleman when we were trying to get the contract. Don had been telling me in previous meetings that he loved Nashville because he went there often to visit his horse in nearby Shelbyville. It was a walking horse - not just any ordinary walking horse, but the world champion walking horse in the particular category in which it competed. While we were meeting one day, his secretary interrupted him with a phone call and Don excused himself and took the call in my presence. I heard him say, "Is he dead?" In my presence he was being notified that this world champion walking horse had died in a fire in the barn where it was housed in Shelbyville, and that call was coming in while I was talking to him and interviewing him relative to a management agreement at his hospital. We developed a real bond and through thick and thin - the board was in a divided position - he always stuck with HMP. I believe that we had a bond which transcended just business but was a personal bond as well.

The point behind this story is, if all things are equal, people "buy" from who they "like" and many times when things are not so equal.

STORY #5

This next story relates to Elkin, North Carolina, which is a lovely textile community with large garment production components. It is a 160-bed hospital in a beautiful area of North Carolina. It is called Hugh Chatham Hospital. Chatham Industries is located there, and it is common that one major industry takes over a particular community and the hospital is often named for that industry. In fact, there is a Chatham descendant on the board of this hospital. We had received a lead that the CEO had died in the spring of 1985 and, though we did not know the exact date, this was considered a very "hot lead." We made a visit to the community, unannounced, and found that the COB and chairman of the search committee was a guy named Fred Edson who had a large oil company based in Elkin. When we arrived, we learned that the CEO had died suddenly of a heart attack and, in fact, he had not even been buried yet. In many instances this could have really offended the board or the community, but they saw it as positive aggressiveness. We ended up meeting with Mr. Edson, developing a relationship and returning after the funeral to make a proposal. He always talked about our management style and how we must be very responsible and aggressive in that we were on-site before the CEO had even been buried. It served as a nice basis for statements about aggressiveness as we managed this very important hospital from May 1985 onward.

STORY #6

This story relates to Saline Memorial Hospital in Benton, Arkansas. This is a 100 plus bed hospital, which was signed on June 15, 1984. It is a bedroom community approximately 30 miles south of Little Rock. We were brought in following an indictment for embezzlement and fraud and subsequent imprisonment of the previous CEO. It was a very political environment. The board was chaired by a gentleman by the name of Dr. Porter who was COB and the anesthesiologist at the hospital. There was a lot of controversy over the potential of HMP managing the hospital in Benton, Arkansas.

Thus, on the night of our final presentation in front of approximately 200 people at the ballroom of the Holiday Inn in Benton, Arkansas, it was a very contentious evening with a number of negative comments from the community, from the medical staff, and the board relative to our potential of managing the hospital. This is not unusual, but there was a significantly greater degree of nervousness than we would typically find. The presentation went well, and we were asked questions at several points. None of them were really favorable, e.g., their loss of control and that we were "carpetbaggers" from Tennessee moving into their community to take money back to Nashville. In any event, we knew that the board members, the bulk of the leadership of the board, wanted to retain us and that it was a matter of selling it. In particular, the leader of the board, Dr. Jim Porter, was probably the primary individual supporting us and we were aware of that. So at the end of this two and a half hour contentious meeting, after maybe 50 negative questions toward HMP, I see a hand raised in the back of the room. It is Dr. Porter. I am thinking, "Do not tell me we even lost him now," and he said, "Mr. Krizelman, I have one last question before I close this meeting down." I said, "Yes, Dr. Porter, please go ahead," and in my own mind I was wondering what could he be asking me - I thought that he was the one key friend we had. He said, "Mr. Krizelman, can you tell me what the N stands for on the football helmet of your alma mater?" I thought for a second and I said, "Well, it stands for Nebraska. That is what the N stands for." And he said, "No that is not correct," and I said, "Well, what does it stand for?" He said, "The N stands for "Knowledge." The entire audience started laughing, and it broke the tension in the room. From that point on the situation changed, and we were seen as very human. Later on in a subsequent meeting, Dr. Porter made the motion to retain us with a contract for several hundred thousand dollars which we retained for many, many years. But I cannot forget that important night and the comedy that broke the tension in the room.

The important marketing point behind this humorous story is the concept of the "garbage can or dumping syndrome." In other words, once the audience had expressed their numerous negative thoughts and fears about retaining HMP, they then could move forward and retain us feeling satisfied that they had fully expressed their concerns.

STORY #7

The next story is about Starke Memorial Hospital which is located in Knox, Indiana. This is a 77-bed rural hospital that is not very far from South Bend, Indiana where Notre Dame is located. Politically it was a "hot bed" and was going to be quite difficult to get a management agreement there. A key member of the board, a judge in the community and an owner of a radio station, is a man by the name of Elmo Smith. In fact, he has written books and is kind of a legend in this community. One would not be able to obtain a management agreement at this hospital without his support even though we did have the support of the COB, a man by the name of Dick Binkley, as well as the two key physicians on the medical staff. Elmo Smith was clearly opposed to us and, in fact, would not see us as part of the marketing process. But I would not give up trying to have an interview with him.

Finally, out of desperation, he said, "If you want to show up at my radio station, go ahead and show up, but I do not expect to see you at 4:00 a.m. when I open the station." Sure enough a few days later at 4:00 a.m., I was sitting in front of his radio station in Knox, Indiana when he arrived with a key to open it up and get the station on the air (and in fact be the coordinator of news, weather, music, and information). So, between 4:00 a.m. and 7:00 a.m. he did not speak to me about HMP or our desire to manage the hospital. Instead he had me working everything from pulling stories off the UPI and AP wire service to picking up a broom and cleaning the station. He made very little conversation. He was a very gruff, grouchy old man. Finally, at approximately 8:00 he asked me in a relatively kind voice if I wanted to have breakfast with him. We went to breakfast at 8:00 a.m. and talked about what HMP could do to manage the hospital. At the end of that lengthy conversation he indicated that we could count on his support and, in fact, he would make the motion to retain us, because if the owner of this management company would show up at 4:00 in the morning in the darkness at his radio station in the dead of winter, he must be very passionate about his product. That work ethic impressed Elmo and is what led to our management agreement.

This was a very interesting community. The chief of the medical staff was a national expert in railroad trains and would travel around the United States looking at different trains. He had a collection of photos of trains. His wife was a fairly well-known national healthcare consultant and here they were based in this little town of Knox, Indiana. From a political point of view it was as explosive as any community we had ever been in, but we were successful in the management of this small rural hospital.

Obviously, tenacity is a very important quality in the marketing process and always directly confronting your enemies so that you can either neutralize them or possibly have them as allies. Never avoid those with negative objections.

STORY #8

This story involves Edinburg Hospital in Edinburg, Texas. This is a community in very south Texas near McAllen, not far from the Rio Grande River and close to the major Mexican city of Renosa. We became very close with the Chairman of the Board at this hospital. He was a young entrepreneur named Humberto Rodriquez and he was a third generation Mexican-American. Humberto had the largest taco chip-tortilla factory in the entire Rio Grande area. He had built it from scratch. During the marketing process, he wanted us to experience life in Mexico and in particular the cuisine. He and his wife took my marketing team to Renosa, Mexico for an unbelievable dining experience. We dined on goat, which I believe in Spanish is *chivo*, and the goats were hanging cooked at the entrance to the restaurant. You knew you were going to be happy. We ate this Mexican delicacy along with about 10 other items, none of which I could identify and none of which were comparable to what we would call Tex-Mex food. That and the beer made for a wonderful evening. Humberto and I became very good friends. Unfortunately he went through a divorce and there were many issues related to that. We remained close friends as well as business associates relative to his role as chairman of the board of this hospital - which we signed. He visited Nashville on several occasions and was one of the few board members or board chairmen to ever come to my house, and we remained friends. His business evolved to become a major corporation.

    This was a case in which the board chairman was clearly the leader of the board and, in fact, we identified him as "the board." Thus, from a marketing view one must clearly identify the power structure and market accordingly. This is also an example of where an insider does the selling and the HMP team must include this person in the marketing strategy.

STORY #9

This is a story that relates to Field Memorial Hospital in Centerville, Mississippi. This is a tiny, rural 66-bed hospital that we signed in 1987. The chairman of the board is Dr. Field and the hospital is named for his father, who was also a physician in this very rural, very tiny and impoverished community. It was like stepping back in time over 100 years, because the hospital was a very antiquated facility in a segregated community in the deep south. In fact, there were still "black" and "white" waiting rooms because Dr. Field said the blacks wanted it that way, not him. Here we were with our marketing team meeting with Dr. Field - who obviously was the key individual on the board - and at the end of our first meeting, in keeping with the local hospitality, he said, let me call my wife because I want to have you all for dinner. His definition of dinner was what I knew as lunch/supper. Around noon we adjourned to his house - an enormous plantation home - and met his wife. At his old antebellum plantation home we ate fried chicken, okra, mashed potatoes and were treated with hospitality like I have never seen before. It was the first time in marketing that the client was worried about our hospitality in their community. We signed the hospital and found a young man to be CEO. He remained there for many, many years because the community and the hospital were united. It turned out to be an outstanding environment for him and a hospital that delivered good quality care in this rural area. The marketing was really done by the client who took care of our meals and treated us as guests in their community.

The point behind this story is that we had to be seen as "family" and as part of the community. We could not be seen as "selling" but rather as members of their extended family. Anything else would have been viewed as threatening.

STORY #10

The next story involves Willow View Hospital, which is the only all psychiatric hospital that we signed in the history of the company. It is located in Spencer, Oklahoma, a suburb of Oklahoma City, on a huge spread of land almost like a rural setting. It is a 93-bed facility with approximately half of the beds dedicated to adult psychiatric and the other half to adolescent. We signed the hospital in 1983.

We were brought there by the CEO, a lady who at one time was a secretary in the organization and subsequently married a man who was chief of the medical staff and chairman of the hospital board. He was a psychiatrist by the name of Harold Sleeper, M.D. who had his office on the campus. He controlled all the physician activities. Of course, he was a typical psychiatrist. As I said, he was not only the key physician, chief of the medical staff and chairman of the board but eventually married the then (CEO) administrator who used to be his secretary. He utilized electroshock therapy, and he had a very unusual kind of therapy that he recommended to patients called "auto urine therapy." He recommended, in certain cases, that patients either drink their own urine or inject it, a highly controversial form of therapy - and a very unusual man. As a result of divorce proceedings with his wife, a story hit in Oklahoma City and national newspapers that revealed facts about how he ran this hospital during this time and administered this unique auto urine therapy - which, it came out in court, he had been administering to his wife. It was a very, very acrimonious and hostile divorce case. The board finally took control of the hospital with our assistance as managers of the hospital. After the divorce, he married the lady who was his administrator. He was disgraced after these public disclosures and he and his new wife moved to Hawaii to never be heard from again.

The point behind this case is that much of marketing relates to the credibility we bring to a new setting. In many instances we were retained so that a board could assure a community that the hospital in essence was hanging out a sign which reads "Under New Management / It's Okay To Visit."

This is a complex example of how, as managers, we had to get the board to terminate its insider couple who together represented the chairman of the hospital board/chief of the medical staff/and CEO of the hospital.

We were successful as contract managers and this hospital became, after a great turnaround, one that we considered purchasing.

STORY #11

The next story involved Kewanee Hospital located in Kewanee Illinois. This is a 111-bed hospital that we signed in 1983. It is a sole provider of a community approximately 90 miles west of Chicago. It is known as the "Hog Capital" of America which is probably self-explanatory. The chairman of the search committee who we worked with was from the supply side for the hog industry. The community had as one of its residents a lady named Maribelle Stewart who in the early 80s was on the talk show rounds including Johnny Carson and all the other major shows. Her specialty was etiquette. She was a modern day Emily Post - an expert. Because she lived in this community and as a favor to HMP, when we had our management conference at the Del Coronado Hotel in San Diego, she agreed to come give a talk on etiquette particularly as it relates to dining. It was held in the ballroom of the hotel for about 200 of our CEO's and their spouses and was a farewell lunch on the last day of the conference. There was a very complicated table set-up for each person - glasses, plates, and particularly silverware. Maribelle talked us through this scenario, and it was almost like she was a straight person in a comedy act. All around the room we had microphones so the CEO's and their spouses could ask her questions. It turned out to be one of the most hilarious events in the entire history of our company. She was a great sport. Remember that at the same time she is appearing on the Johnny Carson show, she is doing this special favor for us - just because she happened to reside in Kewanee, Illinois.

A year or so later it was reported to us that Maribelle Stewart was involved in a very weird act in which she was wearing a rain-coat with no clothes on under it. I believe that was the end of her talk show circuit.

The point behind this unusual story is that a hospital is a community-wide asset and thus you are marketing multiple groups to include the board, medical staff, hospital employees and the community population. It is this interaction with the "community" which provides so many unusual stories and the greatest challenge in the complex marketing of a full-service management contract to a community sole provider general hospital.

STORY #12

The next story involves eating as part of the marketing process. As part of the marketing of Delta Medical Center in Greenville, Mississippi in 1989, we often ate at Doe's Eat Place, a restaurant in an old house. You enter the house through the kitchen. They really only have four things on their menu. They have salads with dressing; they have steaks that vary from 2-5 pounds; they have greasy fries and, of all things, they have tamales. People come from literally as far away as Memphis and other large cities many hours drive away to eat at this institution. One of the highlights of our marketing was to take Tom Singleton, a tremendous steak eater, there along with members of the board/medical staff. Even Tom had trouble with the size of the cuts of meat. I can remember him sitting down one night and devouring a 36-ounce steak after one of our marketing presentations. So Doe's Eat Place is as much a part of the marketing of Greenville, Mississippi as any other thing we did.

There are numerous examples of unusual settings where we ate as we traveled the nation marketing for HMP. The point behind this story is the very "social" nature of eating and the importance of its role in the marketing process, whether it be a Pizza Hut in Shattuck, Oklahoma, a fancy French restaurant in Naperville, Illinois or the example above in Greenville, Mississippi. The "social" aspect of eating in a less-threatening setting than a formal board room provided a less-structured setting for us to make a sale.

STORY #13

The next story involves the hospital in Bentonville, Arkansas, which is Bates Memorial Hospital. This is a small 63-bed hospital signed in 1990 located in northwestern Arkansas. Bentonville is famous because it is the world headquarters for Wal-Mart. It is the home of Sam Walton and all of his family who have lived there many generations.

One of the most memorable events was the sickness and eventual death of Sam Walton. He was in a standard hospital room where he lay terminally ill and where his wife would sit outside his room every day. I can still see her sitting outside the hospital room and being there for him every day. No additional hired nurses, just the normal staff. At that time he was probably the richest man in the world. It was a great example of life, and showed how death seems to equalize everyone when it comes to a terminal illness. This was the wealthiest man in the world and he is dying in a hospital room in a small rural hospital in northwestern Arkansas when he could have been at any famous medical center in the world. It was a real statement about honesty and how this man not only lived his life but really how he was going to die. There is a lot to learn in this lesson.

When we would visit this community during the marketing days and stay at the local hotel, we would see people from around the world who represented major corporations in the United States and elsewhere who were calling on the Wal-Mart corporation to sell their products. The one thing that we learned there is what tough deal-makers they were at Wal-Mart, how they ran their business, and how they purchased items at the cheapest price. We learned that because there was always a number of the Wal-Mart corporation's senior staff on the board of Bates Memorial Hospital, and because the hospital also was run in a very frugal and fiscally responsible manner similar to what we saw in the Wal-Mart corporation.

Thus, in many communities we were exposed to some of the greatest managers and leaders of major corporations in the U.S. Not only did we learn from these executives, but they also very much appreciated our disciplined marketing process. By outlining this disciplined marketing process up front, we set a good example as to how we would manage their community hospital with discipline comparable to their own business skills.

STORY #14

The next story involves the situation in July of 1981 after we started HMP. We would drive everywhere because we did not have the money to fly. In fact, we did not even have a company car, but did have a red Mazda four door which, unfortunately, did not have air conditioning. Tom Singleton and myself left early one Sunday morning in July of 1981 to head to Opelousas, Louisiana - a 13-hour drive. (Incidentally, when I picked Tom up to begin this trip his wife, Sylvia, mentioned that Tom liked to sleep in automobiles and in some instances while he was driving. That statement insured that I would always drive on the long trip with Tom as a passenger.) In addition to Opelousas, we were heading to Houma, Louisiana and then to Arkansas City, Kansas and on to Omaha and then back to Nashville - a trip that was going to take us out of the city for about 12 days straight. As we entered Alabama early that Sunday morning at a rather high rate of speed, we had the fuzzbuster on but were clocked by the Alabama Highway Patrol. They were coming from the opposite direction and by the time we heard the buzzer go off we could not stop in time and, in fact, literally just hit our brakes. The Alabama Highway Patrol gave me a ticket and, as is their custom, to ensure payment they confiscated my driver's license and gave me a little receipt which I could exchange for my driver's license after I had made payment for the speeding ticket. So, that was somewhat disconcerting. Later, we were just inside the Mississippi border and had the trusty fuzzbuster on and were speeding again, and once again the Mississippi highway patrolman was coming the opposite way. The fuzzbuster went off (this is about an hour after the ticket in Alabama!) and we were pulled over. I was driving and Tom Singleton took the fuzzbuster and put it under the seat. We literally almost stopped in the middle of the highway when the fuzzbuster went off. We were afraid that our rate of speed could get us charged with reckless driving. The patrolman asked for my driver's license and all I could produce was this little piece of paper. He looked at it and could see that only an hour ago I had gotten a ticket in Alabama and he said, "Boy, don't you learn?" Then he said, "Now you go on your way. I'm not going to give you a ticket. I ought to haul you into jail, but you go on your way. I'm going to let you go this time." So, we were very fortunate.

Another speeding ticket incident in these stories about autos and speeding involves south Texas. We were heading from the airport in Harlingen, Texas late at night over to McAllen, Texas - about an hour and a half drive on a two-lane road. I had picked up Steve Mason who had been late coming into the airport in Harlingen, and I was traveling at a high rate of speed. It was about midnight, and I saw the red lights behind me and was pulled over. The highway patrolman asked me to follow him, so I followed him to a gas station in a very small town in south Texas which was totally dark. He knocked on the door, and a man came out who was the Justice of the Peace and who then, in the gas station lobby, held court. There was Steve Mason, myself, the highway patrolman and the Justice of the Peace (who was the gas station owner). He said, "The fine will be $145 cash." I said, "I don't have $145," and he said, "How much do you have?" I looked in my wallet and I had $87. He asked the patrolman if he felt I was repentant. The patrolman said, "Your honor, I believe he is." The judge said, "In light of that, the fine will be the $87 in your wallet as payment in full." So he took all of the money I had and let me go.

One other example happened in 1982 when we were marketing and traveling in Wisconsin. We were coming over a hill, and the highway patrol was sitting on the other side of the hill with radar and he got us. We were in our diesel company car. (That company car ended up having 250,000 miles on it when we turned it in after our lease expired. We had our secretary, Gayle Mitchell, turn it in because it was such an embarrassment.) At any rate, the highway patrolman asked for a credit card. He actually had a credit card machine with the little suction feet. He put it on the hood of my car and ran the credit card through it. I had to pay this fine right on site. So I got the ticket and paid the fine, all in one full sweep when he apprehended us in Wisconsin.

There are numerous stories about traveling that include airplane, rental autos and company autos. The point is that traveling is very difficult, but one needs to disregard travel as a problem and totally focus on the business at hand which is the marketing process. In other words, you cannot "take your eye off the ball" but must keep your focus on the process. Thus, travel has to be seen as incidental to the sale.

STORY #15

The next story involves the hospital in Coffeeville, Kansas, which is about a 140-bed hospital called Coffeeville Community Hospital. It was a contested marketing project between HCA and our company, HMP. The competition between the two companies was at a very high pitch in the early 80s. Unfortunately, we lost this one to HCA.

The operations individual for HCA was Jim Stokes. One of the things that was the hallmark of our company was no fraternization with the enemy, meaning HCA. Typically, when we were on a marketing trip, we would not speak other than just to acknowledge their existence politely. If we were outside of the hospital, we usually would not speak. It was all part of the marketing psychological warfare of no fraternization. After the presentation that each of us gave in the very small community of Coffeeville, Kansas, we went to the Baskin-Robbins late at night to get an ice cream cone and ran into the HCA team that included Jim Stokes. Tom Singleton was with me and he approached the HCA team to say hello and shake their hand. I told Tom it was time to go and that we needed to get into the car and leave, so he never got to do that.

A similar story involves sitting across the isle from Jim Stokes and the marketing guy for HCA, Jerry Wilkes, on a flight to Boston. We were on our way to go against HCA in a marketing project at a hospital outside of Boston (where we eventually were unsuccessful). In all of first-class there were only four people: myself, John Smalley from HMP, Jerry Wilkes, and Jim Stokes. Of course, given our policy of no fraternization, we did not speak. The whole principle behind this story is that they were the enemy, no fraternization. Another one of our methods of psychological warfare was to leave the door open during our presentation so that the competing company could hear our booming voices down the hall and then have to follow us in. That could be somewhat intimidating. Another tactic we used in a marketing presentation was to outline to the audience the features to look for in a good hospital management company and how to evaluate the company. If the audience answered the questions properly as presented, it would be obvious that there could only be one solution - HMP, because we designed a very specific set of questions that we put on an overhead in front of the group.

STORY #16

The next story involves the hospital in Port Sulfur, Louisiana, which is a very, very small 50-bed hospital called Plaquemine Parish General Hospital. This is back in 1980 when I was still working for HAI as an operations individual responsible for Louisiana. I was working on this project with a marketing character by the name of Don Knobler. This hospital was approximately 70 miles south of New Orleans. One would think that you could not go further south than New Orleans but you can on a this small peninsula. It is probably the most southern spot in the United States except for Florida.

This hospital had an average daily census of two. It is located in one of the wealthiest parishes (counties) in America because of its oil reserves and other minerals. The family that controlled this area was the Perez family. In fact, the late Leander Perez was one of the leading segregationists in the United States. He had two sons: one was the head of the Police Jury (parish commissioners) and the other was District Attorney. Together, they controlled this parish. Given this background, the hospital would not accept African-Americans and, consequently, did not meet the qualifications for Medicare.

However, the chairman of the board, a lady named Ethel Bailey, believed that they needed to integrate the hospital, get Medicare acceptance and bring the hospital into the twentieth century. So she was the leading proponent behind signing a management agreement with what was then HAI. Theirs was a very inadequate, very primitive hospital covered with shutters to deal with the multiple hurricanes. After we had made our presentations, Don Knobler, quite a character, held up a can of coca-cola and said, "Just like coca-cola, we at HAI are the real thing." Obviously, it was embarrassing but he was a character and they did agree to sign a management agreement. When we returned to get the signatures done, we found that advance warnings were in place for a hurricane to hit that area. We were rushing to beat the hurricane and be allowed to travel down this small peninsula before it was blockaded. We just made it before the hurricane hit and got the signature on the contract. In fact, the hospital was hit by a hurricane and there was some damage. At any rate, we managed this hospital for approximately a year or two, and we increased the average daily census of from 2 to 3 to 50%. But it was very tough going, and it was almost impossible to recruit a physician or a CEO to this primitive hospital. Yet this lady had a vision to open it to the black population and to all others, and we were able to get Medicare approval. It did see the fall of the Perez family who were indicted on some separate issues and, in fact, were put out of power and in prison after their conviction for stealing from the public coffers and election fraud.

At all times during the marketing process, we had to be concerned for our safety and security given the history of this area of Louisiana. Nevertheless, our focus needed to be with the chairman of the board who wanted to open this hospital to everyone and provide quality medical care to the citizens of this wealthy parish (county) where only a few shared in the wealth.

STORY #17

The next story involves the hospital in Sheffield, Alabama. This is about a 200-bed hospital that we marketed in about 1986. The name of the hospital is Helen Keller Memorial Hospital. We were not successful. They decided to remain independent/free standing.

I went on this project with Bobby Huseby, my business partner. One of the things that they were very sensitive about was their heritage and living in the deep south. In introducing the marketing team, I decided to identify Bobby Huseby as being from the area around the Canadian border rather than from his hometown of Duluth, because these southerners did not have any negative feelings about Canadians, but they did about Yankees. The concept here was to be disarming and to respect their local sense of history.

When Bobby Huseby and I worked together (which we did often - as well as with Tom Singleton), self-deprecating humor was always one of the cornerstones of our marketing style. People often talked about how this Shelly was really a guy over six feet tall but over the years they kept beating me down. The best kind of humor is self-deprecating humor. All audiences relate to that and from a marketing point of view, there is a natural gravitation to that approach.

Humor and the ability to laugh at one's self are qualities that people look for when making a major decision to allow us to manage their community hospital. We were guests in their household.

STORY #18

The next story involves the hospital in Arkansas City, Kansas, which is 150-bed hospital called fittingly Arkansas City Memorial Hospital. It was one of the original six contracts signed by HMP and the CEO was Steve Mason. It previously was managed by HAI and with the creation of HMP on July 1, 1981, it became one of the original hospitals in the HMP family.

This is an example of marketing where you become very close to one key individual, in this case, Robert Clark, the COB, who was an official of the key bank in town. We basically utilized our relationship with him as a liaison with this client. I had both a marketing role and an operating role here in the early days and Bob Clark became a very close friend of mine. In fact, he and his wife and daughter came to Nashville and stayed with us. His wife was Judy. He was a very interesting guy because he held the notes at his bank on many of the farms in the area and became a "collection" guy when there would be a default on a note. Often he would take farm implements and other assets to satisfy the note.

When I went to Arkansas City, Kansas, I always stayed with Steve Mason, our CEO, at his house or at Bob Clark's house which was very unique because his hobby was woodworking. He had taken an old house from the turn of the century and redone it into a Victorian house with all restored furniture. One of our rituals when I came to Arkansas City, Kansas was to head approximately one hour south into Oklahoma and go to a restaurant in Ponca City, Oklahoma with Steve Mason, Bob Clark and myself, called Chick & Millie's, where they probably had the best ribs I've ever had in my life. This is an example of marketing built on a strong relationship between our company and the chairman of the board who really controlled this particular board. There was a lesson to be learned from our experience, i.e., the longer the key decision makers have been together, the more you are going to know their patterns.

Ironically, at the end of Steve Mason's assignment as CEO, our replacement CEO turned out to be a "weasel" and "sleazy" and caused us to lose the contract. The board stuck with him and we should have insisted he be terminated. Our fate was tied to this incompetent guy and we let the board influence us to keep a bad guy.

The point is you learn from negative experiences even more than from positive ones. The marketing process does not end with the signing of a contract. When there are problems, the marketing individuals are re-introduced to help solve the problem, or the COB at the time of signing the contract contacts the marketing representative. Consequently, marketing can never be seen as a function separate from operations but as a part of the same team with the operating people.

STORY #19

The next story involves Seventh Ward General Hospital in September of 1986 a 200-bed hospital in Hammond, Louisiana, a community north of New Orleans on the other side of Lake Ponchatrain. It is a parish (county) hospital and as such is filled with all sorts of politics. It is a very interesting community with antebellum homes and very politically sophisticated citizens. We had a great CEO there in Jimmy Cathy.

This situation is an example of when there is one key member of the board who thought hiring a contract management firm, HMP, was a good idea and his name was Dr. Paul Vega. He was a physician and a surgeon. He not only had the leading practice in town, but he also was on the faculty of Tulane and was the medical director of the nearby charity hospital, Lallie Kemp. The marketing here involved Paul. He was a very autocratic, difficult kind of a human being so when you were marketing someone like this, you were only as good as he was. He was both a positive and a negative for those that liked him and for those that didn't like him. There were five members of the parish hospital board and it was, as I said, a very politically charged community. Some people on the board liked Dr. Vega and some people didn't. He did get this contract for us. He did not want any other bidders so he presented it under a Louisiana law which required that there be a bid for a management agreement, and it could only be one year in length - the first year would be a management agreement and succeeding years would be a management assistance agreement. That was his way to make sure we were in. Also, the law required us to run an ad in the newspaper saying that the hospital was about to engage us and that there was a 60-day period during which any other company had the right to make an offer. But we knew this was going to be our project. This was a very interesting project where you live and die by your key guy. In this case he wasn't even chairman of the board, though he had been chairman in previous years. He was the individual who really drove, not only the board, but the medical staff and the whole employment compliment.

STORY #20

The next story involves the hospital in Towanda, Pennsylvania. It is called Memorial Hospital and it is a 99-bed hospital. The hospital was signed by HMP in May of 1987. We used to always stay at a B&B in town - a very beautiful bed and breakfast. The owners rode motorcycles. One of their hallmarks was always to do cross country trips on their motorcycles. They were very unique people who wanted a different way of life. This community had two competing medical groups which were at each other's throats all the time. The unique part about this was marketing this project while this war was going on, because if one group wanted black, the other group wanted white. They pretty well had divided the hospital in a very unfortunate manner. We tried to befriend both groups and that was a very difficult process. In this marketing process, the principal focus of the project was to be friends with both. At any rate, it was a difficult process because if one side felt we were friendly to the other, then the other side would oppose us. In any event, one of our most successful accomplishments was to gain the trust of both groups and make them believe that only a third party such as ours could bring some reason and sense to the management of this hospital. That is exactly what we did, and we were awarded the contract.

After we began managing the hospital, it became our most difficult one because both groups were threatened by us and no matter what decisions we made, one of the groups was at odds with us. It ended up, from an operating viewpoint, being one of the most difficult projects we ever had in our history. From a marketing viewpoint we were successful in obtaining the contract. In many instances a third party can often accomplish things that the existing "players" are not able to.

STORY #21

The next story involves the situation in the community of Vandalia, Illinois and the story of prejudice as it plays out in the marketing scenario. Vandalia, Illinois is the home of a 220-bed hospital, Vandalia Medical Center. It is in Southern Illinois, and the COB, John Staunton, was a major farmer. I worked on this project in 1983 and sold the concept of contract management to both him and the board. But we had two items working against us. One was that after we had sold the concept and had made our presentation first, the hospital said that they wanted another company to come in to present. In marketing the last "guy" in will typically be the winner in a head-to-head marketing competition. You basically want to hold out your competition or have an understanding with the board that you are the only company they're looking at. You don't want a hospital to have your proposal and maybe two weeks later look at another proposal. In other words, you want exclusivity.

That is exactly what happened in this situation with an HCA marketing person. He, in fact, used to work with my partners and me at Hospital Affiliates in the same position, and after HAI was acquired by HCA, he joined HCA and became, of course, a competitor of ours. In the end we lost this project because of the "last guy in" concept in marketing, but also because of prejudice and anti-Semitism. Some blatant anti-Semitic comments were made by the marketing individual about me and about our company to the board in this rural area of Southern Illinois which probably did not have any experiences with Jewish people and certainly had no Jewish members in the community. It was overt, it was blatant, and it was prejudice directed at me and our company. Bob Huseby called the CEO of the management company at HCA to report this incident. It was one of several instances over the years in which this technique was utilized, sometimes successfully, and but most times it backfired. In the end, the main reason HCA got this project was the fact that we had sold the concept. You always make enemies when you have sold the concept, and then the board allows the competition to come in after us. The last group in will always look good. They already know your fee, and they already know what you proposed, and it makes it almost impossible for the first company in to be successful. It is different from when there are two or three companies presenting to the board on the same night. When a competitor comes in two to three weeks afterward, when they know your proposal and know the fees, and when the first company in has deflected all the criticism about the concept of contract management, it always makes the first company look pushy and it makes enemies, and then the second company walks in and takes the project.

The point is that from a marketing viewpoint one must have exclusivity or, if not, a level "playing field" with the other competitors.

STORY #22

The next story involves the hospital in Houma, Louisiana. In mid-1981, we marketed this project. It was a hospital that was already with Hospital Affiliates so after the merger with HCA, they had a right to either exit and go independent, go with HCA, go with HMP, go with some other organization or pursue some other option. This 250-bed multi-specialty hospital was known as Terrebonne Parish Hospital and Alex Smith, the CEO, had been the CEO for HAI, but he did not have a non-compete agreement. The COB was a man who was in the oil recovery equipment business. This was a project that we worked on very hard in July, August and September of 1981. In fact, we went against HCA here, and they could not figure out how we were always there, because we did not have money to fly. They would say, "They're the company that works out of the trunk of their auto."

This is a marketing principle which really comes into play when there is so much competition and so much conflict. This was a hospital that was already with contract management that I had sold earlier when I was at HAI. They were being torn by HCA, HAI, and they had a strong administrator who was really going to have the greatest impact on their decision. They didn't go with either HCA or my company, HMP. Instead they chose Carolina Health and Hospital Corporation (CHHC) out of Charlotte - a company that wasn't even in the fray yet they liked the concept of contract management. Often in marketing when there is that much conflict between two parties, you'll see a hospital select either a third party or stay independent. This really is the principle that was at play here.

STORY #23

The next story involves Rutherford Hospital located in Rutherfordton, North Carolina. It had about 150 beds and it was signed in mid 1983. Over many months we made many marketing trips to this very, very fine hospital. But in the end we would not sell them on the concept of contract management, and they went ahead and selected an executive search firm. In fact, they went through a multi-month process, selected a CEO through the search firm, and set up a date for that individual to start. They had gone through all the candidates, selected this individual, and when it came time to report, the new CEO called and indicated he was not going to take the position because his wife did not want to move to that area.

The marketing principle behind this is that the board turned to our company HMP because, throughout the marketing process and the follow-up process, we were professional. During the follow-up we had stayed in constant contact with the board. When they did not have a new CEO, when he withdrew, they called us and talked to us and, in fact, we signed the management agreement. This goes back to the concept of being professional, being courteous and selling the concept and then following up with the client on a continual basis, even when not selected. We did this and in the end the board selected HMP. It is a great story in which tenacity and professionalism prevailed.

One must take the "high road" even in defeat because the professionalism displayed may result in a future business opportunity as this example shows.

STORY #24

The next story involves Salida, Colorado, which is a small hospital with the name Heart of the Rockies Regional Medical Center. The area around Salida has mountain peaks that are 9,000 to 12,000 feet. This is a small 50-bed hospital which we signed in August of 1985. This story is an example of what we won't do to get a deal. I guess that is the part of the marketing concept related to tenacity.

Salida was a major train center earlier in the century. I remember most vividly wanting to get the deal done because I had difficulty breathing due to the altitude. I would lay in the bed at my hotel room and try to catch my breath. The drive to and from the Denver airport, often made at night, was about 3 1/2 hours. Along the road, as you got close to Salida or leaving Salida, there were elk, sometimes even herds of elk, that would move onto the road. It was an immense hazard with a lot of people losing their life.

Salida was a marketing project in which we were really competing with the concept of remaining independent with the hospital retaining their own internal management. HMP had no competitor other than some regional medical centers in both Colorado Springs and Denver. So this was an unusual project in that there were no for-profit hospital management companies making proposals but rather non-profit medical centers or the concept of remaining independent. We were successful here in large part because our presentation to the board demonstrated our entrepreneurial spirit as well as the important fact that they were not going to be just part of some regional medical center but would remain autonomous in their community. They would still remain the sole provider community hospital and their identity would not be lost. That was our marketing angle.

This illustrates the important marketing concept of a client maintaining their own independence/identity but also having access to the significant resources at HMP.

STORY #25

The next story involves the community of Valdez, North Carolina where we worked on a 150-bed hospital in the mid 1980's. This is very unique community because it is the home of the Waldensians. This is a religious sect that some time ago, hundreds of years ago, immigrated to the United States from Europe because of religious persecution, and they primarily settled in Valdez, North Carolina and surrounding areas. They were bakers and set up their bakeries in Valdez, which then expanded throughout the Carolinas and became a major entity. The COB was a gentleman that owned a home improvement center similar to what would be a Lowe's or a Home Depot. This marketing project really wasn't a matter of competition from another company, but a matter of whether the hospital was going to stay independent or sign with a management company like ours. This was a premier facility and, unfortunately, we were not successful in our efforts to get a management agreement at this hospital.

In this case the community was very interested in maintaining its unique identity and feared it might be lost with a management agreement. It illustrates how each marketing project is so different and one must listen carefully to what each client wants. There can be no "cookie cutter" approach when marketing a personal service business such as hospital full-service contract management.

STORY #26

The next story involves Affiliated Medical Enterprises known as AME located in Los Angeles. This was an intensive resource division project for HMP. Affiliated Medical Enterprises is a five hospital system for-profit entity with most of the hospitals in Southern California except one in New Mexico. The COB and CEO was a man named Dan Young. In approximately 1988, I was on a cruise ship, 1988 or 1989, and I was playing blackjack at the same table with this man, whom I did not know, and we began talking. He mentioned that he was a healthcare executive and was very interested in my company HMP and how we worked, etc., and he wanted my business card. After I got back to Nashville, I received a call from Dan and he wanted to talk to us about doing some consulting and workout for their system. Tom Singleton and I met with Dan and his senior staff on many occasions and we finally were awarded this important contract to do a workout or, as we called it, the Intensive Resource Division (IRD) implementive consulting. The project was to begin on a given Monday and the Bank of Boston was working carefully with us because the financing for this particular project and the debt was held primarily by Bank of Boston, although it was a consortium of banks. Tom Singleton sent out a team to start this project and we had worked out all the details with Dan Young that we would begin on that Monday. When we got there, Dan Young was not there. There was no evidence of where he might be. His leased Mercedes was found at LAX Airport and Dan had left the country and had gone to the country of Taiwan. (Dan was a man of Chinese descent.) We found out that he had a leased Mercedes, a leased house, leased furniture in the house, and that he was having an affair with his brother's wife. He left the country with this lady, his sister-in-law, and her children also. Basically, he disappeared. In fact, his wife called because she was to have a meeting with him about alimony, and our staff were the individuals that had to tell her that Dan was not around anymore and that, in fact, he had disappeared. We had to give her the bad news.

HMP brought in the forensic auditors - they are like ex-FBI agents - and they did a complete audit right at the beginning of our project. Bank of Boston was very interested in us staying on. They discovered significant embezzlement on the part of Dan Young. Basically he had stolen an enormous amount of money from the company to keep his highflying lifestyle in place. It is believed that at some future time, much later on, his body was found in the bottom of Hong Kong Harbor. In addition to these banks, there were a lot of private investors from Asia that he embezzled from, and they had a score to settle with him. Tom Singleton talks about the fear in the early days of the project - not knowing which people who were still at the hospital were associates of Dan Young and in on the embezzlement. Tom had to terminate many people at the beginning of this project. He tells the story about when he was in the restroom and the lights went off. He asked who was in there and he could hear someone there, but no one answered. He obviously was afraid for his personal safety with the termination of so many of these individuals who were associates of Dan Young.

Just another unusual way of marketing a project. This became a very successful project in which we worked for the bankruptcy attorneys and the banks basically to liquidate the various assets including these five hospitals. We sold them off and did a very professional job, but marketing comes in all forms, and this certainly was a unique project from a marketing point of view and one that none of us will ever forget.

STORY #27

This involves Denver General Hospital in Denver, Colorado. This a major 400-bed teaching hospital affiliated with the University of Colorado School of Medicine. It's an IRD project, intensive resource division project, and it is in the inner city of Denver and serves a disadvantaged population. In 1990, HCA had already been marketing this project heavily. The mayor of the city was a man named Federico Peña who went on to become Secretary of Transportation in the Clinton administration for many years. His chief of staff was a lady named Kathy Archaletta, a very sharp lady, who in fact went on to become his chief of staff in the Department of Transportation in the federal government. It was an important marketing principle to recognize that she was the actual individual who was going to make the decision, and it was very important that she liked us. She told us that she did not like HCA because a giant company like HCA threatened her. We did not threaten her. So in this case, from a marketing perspective, the client wasn't really Denver General Hospital or even the mayor.

It is very important to identify who the client is and, in this case, it was the chief of staff who actually was going to make the decision. When it came time for us to meet with Mayor Pena for the final presentation, Kathy had laid the groundwork having determined that, basically, there was only one company for this contract and it was HMP, not HCA. Mayor Pena was basically certifying her decision. It became one of our most successful contracts. Even after moving to the Department of Transportation, Kathy Archaletta and Federico Pena became references for us whenever we were doing projects in urban areas.

STORY #28

The next story involves Zachary, Louisiana. The hospital there is Lane Memorial Hospital. It is a 146-bed hospital signed on May 1982, and it is a hospital in Cajun country just outside of Baton Rouge, Louisiana. Here was a case in which the CEO brought us in. He was the reason we were there. No other company was involved, and unbeknownst to us, the board, led by a powerful local pharmacist by the name of Johnny LaTard, was getting ready to fire this CEO and elevate the current CFO, Charlie Massey, to be the new administrator. Basically, we were getting a contract not because of the man that brought us in. Oddly enough we found out that because the CEO was going to be terminated, the board thought they would need help in the management of the hospital when the CFO took over the position. They weren't sure whether he could run it on his own.

So the marketing principle here is that you never know why you're going to get the contract. I can remember the key member of the board asking me, "Why do you think we're awarding you the contract," and I said, "Because the CEO brought us in." He basically shocked and surprised me by telling me it was the board's plan and didn't involve the CEO at all. They wanted him terminated. So, you can't assume you know their story. Never get ahead of them. They will tell you their truth. Follow their story. Don't peg them - rather follow them. It is very key to listen to their plan and what their story is and not to assume you know what the story is. Obviously, we felt very bad for the CEO who had brought us in, and we did everything we could to try to find him a position in another setting. It is very, very important from a marketing viewpoint that you don't get ahead of your client as to what the story is.

STORY #29

The next story involves Virginia, Minnesota. The hospital is called Virginia Regional Medical Center. It is a 199-bed hospital. It was signed in August of 1981. It was the first contract in our company of 70 hospitals so it holds a very historic position. We really started the company with this important hospital in the very northern region of the state of Minnesota. The COB was a man named John Clark and he owned a very successful mortuary in the community. He was very important to us. John believed in us and, in fact, later on when there was some litigation by HCA against our company, he appeared in a Nashville courtroom and testified on our behalf. We always listened to him. I think that it is extremely important to listen to your client. He had psychological needs, wants and desires that went far beyond his business so it was very important to listen to him and let him get involved as a participant in the management of HMP. Basically he wanted to share in our growth and success. That was important to him psychologically. Later on in his life, he moved to Japan after selling his mortuary. He lost his job there and, unfortunately, lost his family and ended up committing suicide. The story took a very bad turn.

STORY #30

The next story involves Washington, Indiana, Davies County Hospital. It is a 165-bed hospital that we signed in May of 1989. This is a story about accepting diversity and being tolerant. There was a member of the board who owned a bed and breakfast in the community where we stayed. He and his gay partner ran the B&B. We obviously were very tolerant of their beliefs, understanding the wide range of diversity whereas others who had come into this community were not as tolerant. We stayed at their B&B on many occasions and would see them making curtains for the B&B and cooking food (which I might add was wonderful). The marketing point is to be tolerant and to accept diversity.

STORY #31

The next story involves Trinidad, Colorado. This is a 70-bed hospital which was signed in June of 1991 and it is called Mt. San Rafael Medical Center. This is the only hospital in the community of Trinidad, Colorado. It is known nationally as the sex change capital of America. This is another example where we did not make a value judgment about the client. From a marketing perspective we went after the business. A man named Dr. Binder was an internationally renowned individual (who later ran for the county judge position in Trinidad). He was a very respected physician, and physicians from around the country and other healthcare professionals referred patients to him for evaluation and, if appropriate, to perform sex change procedures. The hospital had a multidisciplinary team that included psychologists, geneticists, surgeons and all sorts of support people once the patient qualified for this type of procedure. In any event, the lesson from a marketing point of view is not to judge people but to conduct our business which was managing their hospital. Like the previous story, one must be tolerant of other's beliefs and accept great diversity.

STORY #32

The next story involves Shattuck, Oklahoma and Shattuck Regional Medical Center, a 100-bed hospital that we signed in 1984. I was sitting in a Pizza Hut in this small rural community in the far western region of Oklahoma with the key physician, Dr. Howard Keith, a very prominent thoracic surgeon who could be practicing anywhere but chose this regional medical center. As many people know, I am very opposed to guns and really don't even care to discuss guns let alone the concept of hunting. We discussed hunting for probably three hours, bird hunting in particular, pheasants and quails. This man was, in a major way, involved in hunting. The moral of this story is bullshitting sometimes pays off, though not often. In this case, it did. In most cases it does not. But this is one instance where one had to be tolerant of someone's views (guns and hunting) and it really did involve bullshitting. It's another example of how one's political views have no place in the business of marketing at this level.

STORY #33

The next story involves Paw Paw, Michigan (in the wine country), and the 184-bed hospital is called Lakeview Medical Center which was signed in September of 1984. It had a very savvy board chairman named Chuck Randall who owned a chain of nursing homes. He really understood the need for a sole provider hospital to have a management company like ours. They had a very highly esteemed CEO as their administrator. They believed in this guy, but the place was going down hill. We supported the board and this guy as long as we could until the hospital encountered very bad financial numbers. The moral of the story is we went with their emotions until they were willing to trust us. From a marketing point of view and an operating point of view, we followed their energy. You can't fight energy. The board's energy was going towards a CEO that they believed in, so we had to go with it until we got all the facts. Ultimately, we refocused their energy, but we had to move very slowly, because if we had attacked this guy, they would have turned against us. The moral of this story is to go very slowly, follow the energy of the board until you have all the facts and can present them. We can, at that point, reverse their feeling. The numbers in this case were turning bad, and they realized they needed to make a change. They have to get to that point. You can't take them to that point, because it will appear as if you are criticizing a CEO that they very much respect.

STORY #34

The next story involves Marlette, Michigan. It is a 91-bed hospital that we signed in October of 1984. Marlette, Michigan is in the very upper part of Michigan. It is, as they say, in the thumb of Michigan. Marketing requires great intelligence about what your competition is doing. The board invited us to visit their hospital and make a presentation. The hospital said that they were talking to us exclusively. One of my colleagues, Tom Beavor, was involved in this project as well as Tom Singleton. Well, when my staff arrived at the Hertz counter in Detroit, they encountered Tom Woodward, the senior marketing individual for HCA. In fact, when they got to the parking lot of the hospital, they noticed his car there. Rather than react negatively to the client, we now had information that the hospital was not looking at us exclusively but were, in fact, secretly looking at HCA, too. We did not act in a way that would show the board that we distrusted them, but instead we went about our presentation and never mentioned it. The next morning our staff ate breakfast in a little restaurant in the town of Marlette. We were told the following day that they were going to award the contract to us. The marketing premise behind this story is that, rather than react negatively when we learned the hospital had violated their promise, we basically went along with what they had said. By being professional and having a good product we were awarded the contract.

STORY #35

The next story involves Lynn, Massachusetts. It is called Atlanticare Medical Center. It is a 320-bed hospital which was signed in December of 1988. This is a case which involved one of the operating individuals on our marketing survey team, who was very much respected and liked by the client. They wanted him to stay and become part of the operating team there. We knew that he could not do the job, but rather than challenge the client, we allowed him to stay for a period of time. We later moved him aside and brought in another individual who was an outstanding operating individual and could really run this hospital. The lesson of the story is do what you have to do to get the operating team in the door. And once inside you can work with the board on an agreed upon plan.

STORY #36

The next story involves Granbury, Texas. This is a small 56-bed hospital called Hood General Hospital in a very rural area of Texas that we signed in October of 1991. This is really an incidental story involving our continual marketing of clients. Every year the hospital hosted a golf tournament and awarded a very large sum of money to anyone that shot a hole-in-one. The CEO had not obtained an insurance policy to fund the prize money, and when someone in fact made a hole-in-one, the hospital had to come up with a way to pay for it. This happened prior to our signing a management contract. Marketing is a very mysterious business, and in this case the situation resulted in the hospital board having to bring in new managers to run the hospital. This incident led to our professional contract management of this hospital in Granbury, Texas, just an odd circumstance involving a golf tournament to benefit the hospital.

The point is that marketing leads come in all "shapes and sizes," and marketers must be open to obtaining leads outside the traditional methods.

As a point of information, three out of four times that HMP was awarded a marketing survey at a prospective hospital, that organization would end up signing a management agreement. Getting the survey was the most important part of the entire marketing process.

STORY #37

The next story involves South Charleston, West Virginia. The name of the hospital is Pick Memorial Medical Center in South Charleston. This was a very small community hospital adjacent to Charleston, West Virginia. We had gone through a period during which we had marketed about four different hospitals (this was in the mid 80s) and we had not been successful. We did sign Pick Memorial which was a very undesirable hospital with no possibility of success. This story will demonstrate that if one ever lets panic get involved in the marketing process, it will absolutely destroy the potential for a good operation, and that happened in this case.

I can remember arriving at this hospital and talking with the CEO who was sitting there smoking cigarettes non-stop and ashes were falling off and burning little holes in his suit. He was a very unsightly individual and a very incompetent administrator. Mr. John Sample was COB at that time. Another member of the board, Ben Paul, was a very influential individual who owned a gas station in town and was really the power behind the throne. Pick Memorial is an example of when we should have walked away. It is an important business lesson to know that saying no is a good decision. Some of the best decisions one makes are when one says no. (The CFO in this hospital killed himself in a company car and we are not sure if it was suicide or accidental.)

At a certain point, from an operating point of view, we decided we needed to exit this hospital after signing it and operating it for a while. We realized it was not possible to be successful here. We did exit and the new COB, Ben Paul, viewed our exit as leaving him and "holding the bag." He also viewed us as the only organization associated with the hospital that had deep pockets, so he and the board filed a RICO lawsuit against us. This is a federal interstate anti-mob kind of law, very inappropriate for this case. But it certainly got our attention because it went into federal court. The case was subsequently thrown out, but we did have to make an appropriate financial settlement to satisfy our early exit. Again, the best decisions you often make as business people is when you say no. This story also demonstrates how panic should never play a role in decision making.

STORY #38

The next story involves Arlington, Massachusetts. This was an IRD project, intensive resource division project, and the name of the hospital was Symmes Hospital. It is a 141-bed hospital outside of the Boston metropolitan area signed in late December of 1989. In fact, it was the first "workout" project that the company undertook. Tom Singleton led a division of the IRD, a division which we created to do "workouts" for turnarounds of troubled hospitals in urban areas. This was taking a risk on the part of the company. The point of this story is the need for a company to take risks that are graduated sensible risks. When we were negotiating the contract, the hospital had hired a team out of Boston, very impressive Harvard trained attorneys, that were very involved in structure and very involved in the technical aspect of contract law. Basically we bowed and let them know how smart they were, but when it was all over, HMP had the business terms that were necessary. The moral of this story is, if they were very content to prove how smart they were, then we were very content to make sure the key issues of the business were maintained.

Another marketing principle is very important here. We really never used attorneys to negotiate the contracts, because attorneys negotiating with attorneys usually ended up with a contract that could take months to execute. Rather, it was our company, as business people, who always negotiated with attorneys for a given hospital. In this way they would not feel threatened by another attorney. In the end, behind the scenes, we had our own attorneys who we could consult with, but it was never attorney-to-attorney. We always allowed the attorneys for the hospital we were negotiating with to prove how smart they were, and we were content to be in the background while they proved that.

STORY #39

The next story involves Phoenix, Arizona and Phoenix General Hospital, a 91-bed hospital signed in December of 1988. This is an interesting story of tenacity. Both HCA and HMP had made proposals to manage this hospital in the heart of Phoenix. The hospital selected HCA and went about the business of negotiating the contract. HCA assigned their chief legal counsel to work with the board and its attorney. From time to time we would follow up on this case to see whether the contract had been executed. The hospital and HCA actually installed their administrator without a final contract, a lady name Joanne Castrena, who had previously worked for me at HAI. She was a very talented individual who was a nurse by training and had become a hospital administrator. So, they had placed a good team in there but negotiations were still going lawyer to lawyer. A month went by, two months went by, and still no contract. The bottom line was that they made it such a negative contractual negotiation that they never got the contract done. The hospital stopped negotiating with HCA and negotiated a contract with our organization within 24 hours. HMP ended up managing this hospital after HCA had been awarded the account but could not get a contract done. The moral of this story is never to allow lawyers to negotiate for you - it will be seen as a legal transaction rather than a very human business transaction.

STORY #40

The next story involves a two-hospital system in the Los Angeles metropolitan area called Triad. It was an Intensive Resource Division hospital. This story is an example of how you never know who your client is going to be. "Out of the blue" we received a call from Stuart Marylander, a very respected CEO, who previously had been the CEO of the prestigious Cedar-Sinai Medical Center in Los Angeles. Stuart called us and we respected him as the client. We never tried to go around him to the board. In turn, he presented our credentials to the board and subsequently we met with them. This is a marketing story about understanding who your client is. In this case, it was this very well-respected administrator who, in fact, did retain us on behalf of the board. We had a successful project at this organization because we understood who the "customer" was.

STORY #41

The next story involves Albion, Michigan, Albion Community Hospital. This is an 81-bed hospital outside of Detroit which we signed in November of 1982. This is an example of learning, after signing this hospital, that it was performing an unusual medical procedure called Mason-Shunt procedure - stapling the stomach as a modality to reduce the weight of obese people. There were serious medical quality issues that we did not know about on the front end. Even though it may have been an accepted procedure, it was being done too frequently and by two brothers who were not experts. We were not making a judgment about the Mason-Shunt stomach fat reduction procedure, but rather a judgment based on the quality of care at this institution. The moral of this story is that you can't be associated with bad quality of care. After a period of time, we exited this organization because of these concerns.

In this business you are judged by the "company" you keep and quality references are the best marketing tools.

STORY #42

The next story involves Berlin, Maryland. The name of the hospital was Atlantic General Hospital. This hospital was signed in September of 1991. It was a 62-bed hospital that was being planned for the shore of Maryland. Basically, a brand new hospital was to be constructed in this huge growth area that had not had a hospital before. We were to build it, manage it and staff it. It was a major project. This community and their board felt it was necessary to retain a very prestigious law firm to negotiate the contract which they did. They retained the law firm of Jaworski based in both Washington D.C. and Houston. Jaworski had been the former Watergate prosecutor during the Nixon administration. The bottom line was that this prestigious law firm was very over-qualified for contract law. Here is another example from a marketing point of view in which we allowed a law firm to prove to us how smart they were. This became the most difficult legal contract we had ever negotiated, and yet we kept our cool. Finally, when the contract wasn't getting done, we had to go to the COB to let him know that the board was going to have to get involved or there was not going to be a contract, and also that they were spending more money per hour, per week and per month with this law firm than for our contract fee. The law firm was charging them $500/hour per person. Finally, that got the board's attention. They made some decisions and "encouraged" the law firm of Jaworski to finalize the contract quickly which they did. We went on to build the hospital, recruit the staff and manage the hospital in this resort area of Maryland.

STORY #43

These next stories involve a few of the disasters we have encountered over the years during various management responsibilities. They characterize, from a marketing point of view, the awesome responsibility you have when you execute a contract to manage a hospital. Two of our management contracts involved hurricanes. One was at Beaufort Memorial Hospital, a 99-bed hospital on the outer shore of South Carolina that we signed in July 1985. Another was in Morgan City, Louisiana involving Lakewood Hospital, a 78-bed hospital signed in April of 1992. Both of these facilities were damaged and both of them had to activate the disaster plan under our direction.

We signed a management agreement in March 1990 in Petersburg, Virginia at Southside Regional Medical Center, a 468-bed hospital. There was a major fire at this hospital and unfortunately several people lost their lives.

These three examples of disasters are included to demonstrate the marketing responsibility and awesome management leadership responsibility one assumes when taking responsibility for total and complete management of a hospital. There is a bond between you and that community to protect it at all costs.

STORY #44

The next story is a personal story about the tenacity and courage necessary to begin a company and handle its marketing as one of the founders. We began HMP on July 1, 1981. In 1982, I developed a very bad chest cold and went to a physician who determined that my lungs were filling up with mucus. He needed to not only give me cough medicine and an antibiotic, but to really knock it out, in his judgment, I needed adrenal cortisone steroids. In fact, it did knock out my illness. But it resulted in a very rare and unknown side effect - a disease called avascular necrosis. This is basically the dying of many joints in the body that can't get access to blood supply. It is like having a heart attack of the joints. This all just happened innocently by a physician prescribing medicine - something called a dose pack by Upjohn Pharmaceuticals with declining dosages taken orally over a seven day period. My lungs cleared up, but it was like using a sledge hammer to kill an ant. When I developed some of these very rare unknown complications, our company was about a year old. I was trying to determine how to still function and walk and carry on a brand new business to support my family.

This became a story about tenacity and hopefully courage. The disease first affected my hip, and then spread to all of my joints. I saw the future of the company at risk because it was such a small start-up company and only a year old. I was very scared. I was on crutches. I eventually was sent to Johns Hopkins Hospital where I had an experimental surgical procedure on my hip which was successful. I continued to try to market, and we chartered small airplanes so I could lay down. I was on crutches for six months before the surgery and while it was healing.

This is not so much my story as it is about working with my colleagues like Bob Huseby, Tom Singleton, Tom Beavor and others. They would call me from a particular project like Paris, Illinois, where they would be handling the marketing. I would have to handle it remotely by phone because I wasn't able to travel to some of these places. I'm sure it not only scared me but it scared our families and it scared all the employees and my fellow partners. We all had to keep going though, because so many people, and so many clients, and so many colleagues were depending on all of us as a brand new company.

We had to stay focused on the business/marketing, and as a start-up company, I did not want those around me focusing on me instead of our new business.

STORY #45

The next story involves retaining a new marketing executive who we had recruited from the Marriott Corporation. We got the lead from one of my colleagues, Tom Beavor, who spoke highly of this individual. He had a perfect background with about 20 years selling major contracts for prestigious corporations such as the Marriott Corporation. He began with us in 1985 during our third year of business when we were ready to add a major marketing individual of this caliber. During the interview process and the background check we didn't find anything unusual, only good things. The point of this story is that the complexity of selling contracts to manage a hospital and sometimes being the most focal point in any community with multi-hundred thousand dollar arrangements over many years yielding millions of dollars, is a very complex sales process involving physicians, board, employees, patients, the community and others. It is unlike any sales process of any other product and certainly any hard asset that one would typically try to sell.

After about a two week orientation in the office, we began working with him and allowing him to accompany us. We noted that he kept sniffing his nose and would also need to stop repeatedly to go into a restroom. Finally, before a major presentation in Rolla, Missouri, he started having significant nosebleeds, but we did not know the nature of them. This behavior became very unusual. He was with me learning the "ropes" in Rolla. I spent about a week non-stop with him and became concerned about his strange behavior. I felt that the constant nosebleeds were also very troublesome. Then he went onto a project in Clarksville, Arkansas where we were working to sign a contact at the same time we were in Rolla, Missouri. He accompanied Tom Beavor to learn about the marketing and see a project presentation at Johnson County Regional Medical Center. There his nosebleeds continued, and he began sleeping during interviews and presentations to the board. This behavior was very aberrant and it became necessary to send him back to his home in the Washington D.C. area and, in fact, to get him on a plane from Little Rock to Atlanta and on to D.C. We were called by the nursing staff at Hartsfield Atlanta International Airport where he was found wondering around the airport. We called his wife and she came to get him. I was sure that he would have to be hospitalized. We had someone working for us with a cocaine problem. The point of this story is that from a marketing point of view we probably had a cocaine user here who thought he could manage his life with modest amounts of cocaine, but when the stress became so huge selling something as complex as our product, he probably increased his usage and, in fact, got into trouble. That is our best reading on the situation. Obviously, he was terminated. One doesn't know this when they are interviewing someone and checking them out and talking to all of their references. Probably it was the nature of this new position with our company and its complexity that pushed him over the edge.

Nevertheless, people were our most valuable asset in the company and it was important to protect the credibility of all our employees and their important fiduciary role with potential client hospitals.

STORY #46

The next story is the most important marketing story of all because it is the spring of 1992 and we had our company for just about eleven years and we had made the decision to sell the company. We had looked at both the New York Wall Street firm of Bear-Stearn as well as J.C. Bradford in Nashville to sell our company, HMP. We selected J.C. Bradford's Merger & Acquisition people (Bob Doolittle) to handle the transaction for us. After a lengthy process, we were down to two finalists: one was Hospital Management Associates (HMA) in Naples, Florida with the principal officer Bill Shoen, and the other was Quorum in Nashville, Tennessee which, of course, had earlier been the management company spin-off of HCA in 1989. We had made a decision to sell our company to Quorum if we could get the right deal. Although we liked Bill Shoen very much and HMA in Naples, Florida, their package for our company was going to be 100% HMA stock (which by the way would have been a tremendous transaction because their stock skyrocketed). But, we needed the security of a transaction that was half cash and half betting on the future via stock and that is what Quorum offered.

I have a very close friend by the name of Ken Melkus who was on the board of Quorum and was also part of the venture capital firm Welsh Carson Anderson & Stowe of New York. This is the firm that put the money, their venture capital money, behind Quorum in 1989. Ken had previously been the president of Surgical Care Affiliates under the chairmanship of my good friend, Joel Gordon. We had had some earlier discussions (approximately 1991) with the CEO of Quorum, Jim Dalton. Those discussions did not go anywhere for two reasons: we did not have a plan in place to sell HMP, and because Jim Dalton could not generate interest with Welsh Carson and specifically the Quorum, Chairman of the Board, Russ Carson.

A year later in the spring of 1992 when Ken Melkus got involved, he wanted to make sure that this transaction got done because he really believed in our company, HMP, and thought that we would be a wonderful fit with Quorum. In fact, he thought we could do a reverse merger whereby our culture and our senior management would come out on top even though Quorum had nearly 300 hospitals and our company only had 70.

During the negotiations in the spring of 1992 we were primarily working with the president of Quorum, Jim Dalton, but behind the scenes we consulted with Ken Melkus when there was an impasse, and we would try to get more money in the deal for HMP. We had gone on two previous occasions to Ken Melkus and he in turn had gone to Russ Carson, the COB of Quorum and a partner at Welsh-Carson-Anderson & Stowe, and had basically got done what we had wanted done.

Then on a particular Thursday in the month of May 1992, my partner, Bobby, asked me to use my friendship and go one more time, the third time, to Ken Melkus. I did do that and Ken Melkus said that not only was there no more money and nothing we could add to the deal, but by 3:00 p.m. tomorrow, meaning Friday, our deal will be pulled off the table from Quorum and there will be no deal left. Of course, at the time we were still looking at the offer from HMA so this was a pretty big shock. We had taken it to the edge and even Ken had balked in the end and said that was everything there was. That was the deal!! Well, the next afternoon prior to 3:00 p.m. we called Jim Dalton and told him that we had accepted the deal. We knew that there was no more money in the deal and we had gotten every cent.

Actually, this had been the biggest marketing project of all and put our marketing skills to the test because this was the ultimate deal. Of course, the deal did get done. The transaction closed on July 1, 1992. I can still remember receiving a check for the cash in the transaction and the stock.

To this day, I am very close to Ken Melkus, and I always joke with him that we left a lot of money on the table. Ken always starts laughing and tells everyone that not only did we get a good deal, and not only did we not leave any money on the table, but we also took the table. He loves to tell the story. In a more serious vein he also tells people that our merger allowed Quorum to "go public" and trade for as much as $35.00 per share. When the stock was given to us, it had a fair market value of only $2.50. This was a wonderful deal for HMP and its employees/families.

The point behind this entire story is friendship and how that trust played a role in taking the deal to another level and having an insider on the board. This was different from when we were selling a management contract and an insider got the deal done. The same principles that applied to us successfully getting a management contract also applied to the sale of our company and getting this successful deal done. Obviously, for any deal to be truly great we had to perform and provide value for our stockholders. During our management era the stock went from $2.50 to $35.00 per share.

STORY #47

The next story involves a retreat hosted by the New York venture capital firm, Welsh Carson Anderson and Stowe, which put up the money for Quorum and was really behind the acquisition of our company, HMP. This was in late summer, early fall of 1992, about three or four months after the successful sale of our company, HMP, to Quorum, one of the firm's under the control of the venture capital firm. They were having the retreat at the Greenbrier Resort in White Sulphur Springs, West Virginia, and it was for the companies that they had invested money in. Welsh Carson at the time had invested money in about 50 companies. About 25 of those were management information system companies and the other 25 were healthcare companies. Welsh Carson wanted to develop some synergy among the 25 healthcare companies so that we could, so to speak, cross-fertilize with one another and basically refer business and other activities within the "family."

Bobby and myself, being the "new boys on the block," went to our first meeting with all the CEO's of the 25 healthcare companies from Welsh Carson Anderson & Stowe, including Quorum and its president, Jim Dalton. Ken Melkus, Quorum board member, attended because he was also one of the principals of Welsh-Carson-Anderson & Stowe. Russ Carson (Senior Partner & Quorum COB) wanted to get a feel as to the level of healthcare knowledge in the assembled audience of these 25 CEO's and the other senior people from these companies. He asked everyone to raise their hand who had been in healthcare for five years, then for ten years, and for fifteen years and for twenty. Finally, at 25 years, after this whole process, Bobby Huseby and I were the only two individuals with our hands up. Russ Carson asked, "Well how about all those that have had 25 years of experience or more?" Of course we were very proud of the fact that we had more healthcare experience than anyone in the room. Ken Melkus was sitting next to me. He said, "You know what is amazing to me Shelly?" And, of course, I was so proud that we were still holding our hands up. Ken said, "That you could be in this business for 25 years and know so little - it is just so amazing to me," and he started laughing. We just have that sort of friendship. He is like a proud father who to this day still talks about the transaction with HMP and how it was the turning point at Quorum providing the opportunity for Quorum to go public and grow and become over a one billion dollar company. He is extremely complimentary, and the base of our relationship and friendship is not only that we performed well, but the humor in our day-to-day activities. He is still proud of that transaction. We not only brought our management expertise from HMP to Quorum, but most importantly, we brought with us a new culture that we rapidly implemented at Quorum.

STORY #48

The story involves joining Hospital Affiliates International (HAI) in 1978. Hospital Affiliates was looking for a senior project consultant, really a CEO, to be the lead individual on a project involving Santa Clara Valley Medical Center, a 667-bed hospital in San Jose, California. It was a teaching hospital affiliated with Stanford University School of Medicine. Santa Clara Valley Medical Center is the county hospital for Santa Clara County, an enormous county which has a significant indigent population, but it also is the home for the West Coast of a 300-bed spinal cord injury center. It is a very prestigious medical center with teaching programs at both undergraduate and graduate levels in connection with the affiliation at Stanford University School of Medicine in Palo Alto, California. At that time, I was the CEO of the University of Kansas Medical Center.

In 1978, I was interviewed by two senior officers from Hospital Affiliates International, Steve Geringer and Tom Cigarran, both based in Nashville. They sought me out at the University of Kansas to recruit as the senior project consultant (CEO) of this medical center. HAI had not secured the contract yet. It was to be decided by a five-member Board of Supervisors - said another way, the county commissioner for Santa Clara County, a county with 3,000,000 citizens. It was a very contentious contract process that HAI was going through. The labor unions, Hispanic groups and various community groups were strongly opposed to turning over the management of this hospital to outsiders. Of course, my career had always been as a solo administrator, without a management company, so this was my first attempt to become part of a multi-hospital system as a CEO for HAI. It was a major career change for me, but I was willing to do it because of what I thought the future would be with multi-hospital management and a management company like Hospital Affiliates. It was also an opportunity to live in Northern California where I had lived previously and to be close to my brother and his wife and their family. It was a very contentious proposal and the Chairman of the Board of Supervisors, a man named Rod Dierdon, a key individual in the Democratic party for Santa Clara County, was strongly opposed to this

$1,200,000 base fee per year consulting contract. On the other hand, the county executive, Bill Siegel, was strongly in favor of retaining HAI. The other Board of Supervisor members were somewhat split as to whether HAI should be retained. There also was a CEO of the Medical Center at the time who we would work closely with, Dr. Anne Russell. So in a way it would be like a dual CEO role. A very complicated arrangement, yet worth doing - if HAI could obtain this major contract.

The two key members of the Board of Supervisors that HAI needed to convince were Ms. Geri Steinberg and Mr. Sig Sanchez. In any event, prior to selecting HAI, a major hearing was conducted in the Board of Supervisor's chambers with the local media present and, in fact, the hearing was televised live on local television in San Jose. It was a major story. Mr. Geringer and Mr. Cigarran from HAI made the proposal and, of course, I was not there because I was in Kansas City awaiting the outcome of the vote. Approximately 40 people spoke in opposition to hiring HAI and only one man spoke in favor - at the end of the presentation. After a very long debate, and testimony and opposition by labor groups, Hispanic groups and community groups, and with a lot of courage, the Board of Supervisors cast a split 3-2 vote to retain HAI for a two year management consulting contract over the objection of the Board of Supervisor Chairman, Rod Dierdon. And, there had been only one individual who spoke in favor of the contract at the hearing.

After Tom Cigarran and Steve Geringer got back to Nashville, I talked with them and asked how it went. They said HAI had been retained and I needed to pack my bags and prepare for moving my family to the Bay area to assume this major project. I asked who the one individual was who spoke in favor. They said that he was a very articulate man. He appeared to be a businessman and spoke at the end of the hearing. They remembered him as a dapper dresser who wore Gucci shoes. I, of course, knew that individual to be my brother. He did not give his name but very eloquently stated his position, as a citizen of the area, that the Board of Supervisors needed to retain Hospital Affiliates International (HAI). Tom Cigarran told me this story and though I knew it was my brother, I did not say anything to Tom.

Many months later when Tom Cigarran was out visiting the account in San Jose, my brother and I were together and I wanted Tom to meet my brother. The first thing Tom said was, "You're the man with the Gucci shoes that testified on behalf of retaining HAI!" So, it was quite a humorous story, which by the way, took place six months later when I finally got the courage to hook up my brother with Tom Cigarran.

Tom Cigarran has gone on to be the CEO of a major publicly traded company and has remained a good friend of mine in Nashville. He is really the reason behind my move to Nashville and the subsequent creation of our three successful companies. I have ways felt that I owe a lot to Tom Cigarran. Every time I see him he always asks how the man in the Gucci shoes is doing. In fact, not too long ago, when I got married, Tom Cigarran was at the wedding and got to see the man with the Gucci shoes again, otherwise known as my brother.

STORY #49

In 1981, two other gentlemen and I founded Hospital Management Professionals (HMP). We had all been senior officers of Hospital Affiliates International. When we left HAI, it had just been acquired on July 1 of that year by Hospital Corporation of America, and we decided not to join the acquiring company but instead to form our own company. We did on July 1, 1981. There were certain "issues" relative to our obtaining new contracts. Six of the hospitals we signed had previously been contracts that we were responsible for when we were at HAI, but the hospitals had no restrictions and we had no restrictions signing contracts with these hospitals. We did not have non-compete contracts. Nevertheless, the acquiring company, Hospital Corporation of America, wanted to send a major message to the three of us.

In the early fall of 1981 they filed a $32,000,000 lawsuit against our new company, HMP, and against the three of us individually. They asked the court for an immediate injunction to stop us from doing business. The three of us were 36 years old, we were married and we had small children. All of us were economizing that summer after starting the new company - not using air conditioning in our homes, no new clothes for us, our spouses or our children, and driving in a company car which was an old Mazda 4-door with no air conditioning. Now we were facing this $32,000,000 lawsuit. In addition, Hospital Corporation of America (HCA) not only sued us and our new company and asked for an injunction, but they sued our six new client hospitals. They were represented by Richard Lansden, a partner in the prestigious law firm of Waller Lansden Dortch and Davis. We hired an attorney that we could not afford to pay on a regular basis, and his name was Stuart Kresge. He agreed to accept stock in our new company in exchange for his willingness to act as our legal counsel. (Incidentally, Mr. Kresge's stock was worth nearly $500,000 when we sold HMP in 1992.) As chance would have it, Stuart Kresge was not a litigation attorney and thought the best approach would be to use an attorney by the name of George Barrett. George was a very prominent attorney who focused on labor and social issues, and he was at the forefront of multiple civil rights issues. He agreed, because of Stu's request, to take our case. So, there was drama in the courtroom when Hospital Corporation of America (HCA) met our little HMP. This was a $20 billion company going against three men who had put $10,000 each into their new business. Hospital Corporation was asking for an immediate injunction and immediate cessation of activity by our company. If they had been successful in the fall of 1981, there never would have been an HMP, and in fact, probably the three of us as well as our company would have been in bankruptcy.

It was an all day hearing held before Judge C. Allen High in Nashville. So, there was this flamboyant civil rights attorney who represented us going against this famous attorney from a very large, conservative, mainstream Nashville firm. In the end the judge denied HCA's request for an injunction and basically the lawsuit disappeared over a period of time. This suit enabled the three of us in our new company (HMP) to be so strong, because we had weathered a lawsuit by one of the largest corporations in the world and had survived. Out of that came great strength, tenacity and courage. As a result, many managers wanted to join our company, because they saw us as the men who took on HCA and won!

IX. ABOUT THE AUTHOR

Sheldon L. Krizelman grew up in Omaha, Nebraska, where he attended public schools and then went to the University of Nebraska for his undergraduate work in Business Administration. He completed his Master's Degree in Hospital Administration at the University of Minnesota and attended the Executive Program at Harvard University. Afterward he served in the United States Army as First Lieutenant in the Medical Service Corps and was stationed at a field hospital in Southeast Asia during the Vietnam War and then at the U.S. Army Specialized Treatment Center at Ford Ord, California. He was awarded the Army Commendation Metal, the Vietnam Service Medal, and the Vietnam Campaign Medal.

Upon completion of his military experience, Mr. Krizelman joined St. Luke's Hospital in Cleveland, Ohio as Director of Operations (COO) and was responsible for the affiliation between St. Luke's and Case Western Reserve School of Medicine. After increasingly more significant positions, including appointment as CEO of the University of Kansas Medical Center at age 32, he joined Hospital Affiliates International (HAI) where he was responsible for the management of Santa Clara Valley Medical Center, a major teaching hospital affiliated with Stanford University School of Medicine. Upon completion of this project, he became Director of Teaching Hospital Projects at HAI. Mr. Krizelman's relationship with HAI enabled him to experience the for-profit sector of hospital management. This relationship eventually led to his move to Nashville which most professionals consider the "Silicon Valley" of healthcare management for the nation, where Mr. Krizelman became a Group Vice President of HAI and was responsible for the operation of 17 hospitals.

After the sale of HAI to a cross-town rival, HCA, Mr. Krizelman was a principal and co-founder of Hospital Management Professionals (HMP) which grew to become the second largest manager of hospitals in the nation. It had 70 hospitals under full-service contract management agreements in 39 states. In addition, he co-founded Health Advantage

Inc. (HAI), a diabetes contract management company which established centers of excellence for the treatment of diabetes in large urban hospitals in several states. Subsequently, he co-founded Healthcare Connections (HCC), which was an organization involved in the management of preferred provider organizations (PPO's) in rural areas. All three of these companies, founded in the early 1980's, were sold in mid 1992. The largest company, Hospital Management Professionals (HMP), was sold to Quorum Health Group in Nashville, and Mr. Krizelman became Executive Vice President of Quorum Health Resources where he remained through the late 1990's. One of the other two companies, Health Advantage, Inc., was sold to a publicly traded company in 1992 and Healthcare Connections was sold to its management. Mr. Krizelman remained with Quorum Health Resources where he was responsible, along with other senior officers, for Quorum becoming a publicly traded company in the mid 1990's. Quorum Health Resources managed or had management assistance agreements with 450 hospitals throughout the United States. In 1996, Mr. Krizelman received the Philip Kotler Award for Excellence in Healthcare Marketing from the American Marketing Association.

In 1999, Mr. Krizelman stepped down from Quorum to spend increasingly more time on community activities to include working for many years with the mayor of Nashville in the role of Board Chairman of the Metropolitan Hospital Authority which was responsible for both Metropolitan Nashville General Hospital and Metropolitan Nashville Bordeaux Hospital. He played the instrumental role in the merger between these hospitals and Meharry Medical College as well as the subsequent affiliation between Meharry Medical College and Vanderbilt University School of Medicine. This was a very unique transaction involving the City of Nashville, Vanderbilt University, and Meharry Medical College.

Mr. Krizelman is a frequent guest lecturer at Vanderbilt University including the Owen School MBA Program, the Owen School Executive MBA Program, and Peabody School. He is the author of multiple articles in professional publications and is a Life Fellow of the American College of Healthcare Executives. Currently, he is very closely involved in the campaign of Phil Bredesen for Governor of Tennessee and the congressional campaign of Jim Cooper. Mr. Krizelman was previously involved in Mr. Bredesen's successful Nashville mayoral election and two terms in office. In addition, he is active as a Board of Trustees member of Meharry Medical College and in many other community and philanthropic activities.

Mr. Krizelman resides in Nashville, Tennessee with his wife, Patricia Kraft Krizelman, and between them they are the parents of four grown children.